THE GRAVEDIGGERS

Beware of a 'once in a lifetime opportunity'.
Although this looks good on the surface things
aren't at all what they should be and the whole
situation could turn rotten very easily. Your
budding romance takes an unexpected turn.

HORROR
S C O P E S

J. H. BRENNAN

THE
GRAVEDIGGERS

MAMMOTH

First published in Great Britain 1996
by Mammoth, an imprint of Reed International Books Ltd
Michelin House, 81 Fulham Road, London SW3 6RB
and Auckland, Melbourne, Singapore and Toronto

Copyright © J. H. Brennan, 1996

ISBN 0 7497 2733 0

A CIP catalogue record for this title
is available from the British Library

Printed in Great Britain
by BPC Paperbacks Ltd

ONE

Andy kissed her.

He felt her stiffen slightly, then relax. For just a moment she was kissing him back, then she pulled away. 'Hey,' she said, 'maybe we should take this a little more slowly.' But she was smiling.

Andy released his grip on her shoulders and looked at her. Even after she'd been pounding guitar for hours, she still managed to look fresh and crisp. That was one of the things he liked about her. One of *several* things he liked about her.

He found himself thinking of the first time he saw her. She walked in on a rehearsal carrying a guitar case and demanding an audition. Dave and Tim weren't keen – they had the idea women weren't cut out for rock – but Andy felt fireworks exploding in his head ... and other parts of his anatomy if he was honest. Sandra was gorgeous. Great hair, great face, great figure. She looked a little like a brunette version of Baby D and, when he overruled Dave and Tim, she showed them she could play guitar like a demon.

Andy made over the entire group in two minutes flat that day. In his head, he saw Sandra up front dressed in tight jeans and an open shirt, something white with frills. She would be slamming that guitar and belting out something really raw from the old days – maybe a Stones number, 'Sympathy for the Devil', something like that.

It was how he saw her, but it turned out there was a problem. Sandra couldn't sing. At least, she *could* sing, but not well enough. Not the sort of voice that would carry the *Gravediggers* to stardom.

But Andy took her on just the same and inside a week even Dave agreed he was right. She looked fantastic in the line-up. When she played it was like she made love to the guitar. The audience couldn't take their eyes off her.

Andy couldn't take his eyes off her either.

He asked her out the second time he met her. She turned him down, but in a way that made it no big deal so he asked again. This time she went out with him – a pizza and Coke after rehearsal. After that the cinema a few times. She kept him at a distance. He had the idea she'd been hurt at some time and had learned to be careful. That was okay by him; he knew about patience. This was the first time he'd kissed her.

Andy grinned at her. 'Slow is good,' he said.

They'd stopped at the end of her street, a tree-lined avenue of old Georgian houses all long since converted into flats. It wasn't very late – the rehearsal had finished by ten – but this was a quiet residential area and there was nobody else about.

'Come on,' Sandra said. 'Walk me to my door.'

She took his arm, which was something she

didn't usually do. They strolled along the pavement with Andy very much aware of her spicy perfume and the soft heat of her body, making him wonder if slow really *was* good. He had the idea he was far more sure of his feelings towards Sandra than she was of her feelings towards him.

To take his mind off it, he said, 'What did you think of the rehearsal tonight?'

'Went well,' Sandra said. 'Dave's much improved. We all are. I'm not sure we aren't ready.'

'Ready for what?'

'Ready for whatever,' she shrugged. 'The big break. Isn't that what all the new rock groups are waiting for?'

'I don't know if it works like that,' Andy said. 'Outside the movies.'

'How do you think it works, Andy?' She stopped walking and looked up at him.

Andy felt a tightening in his stomach. He wanted to lick his lips but didn't want her to see he wanted to lick his lips. She had brown eyes you could drown in and the way she was looking at him made him wonder if he was reading everything all wrong. Maybe he should just invite himself up to her flat for coffee.

Andy swallowed. 'I think mostly it's just slow and steady. If you're good, you gradually get better and better gigs and one day you've built up enough of a track record for a record company to notice you.'

Sandra pursed her lips. 'Andy Clarke, I sometimes wonder if you didn't go straight from adolescence to middle age.'

3

'What?' Andy asked. 'What did I say?'

They had reached the short flight of stone steps up to her front door. 'Gradually get better and better,' she mimicked mockingly, her lips pouting. 'A little bit here, a little bit there ...' She smiled suddenly and broadly. 'What happened to excitement? What happened to adventure? What happened to the luck of the draw, the surprise phone call, the bolt from the blue?'

Andy stared at her in bewilderment. 'Well, I mean, maybe—'

Sandra said, 'I'm psychic – did you know that? I predict you're in for a big surprise soon. One that makes you forget the slow and steady nonsense.'

Andy spread his hands. 'Hey, I hope you're right. I mean, I'd love it to happen that way.'

She stood up on tiptoe and kissed him again, but on the nose and so quickly he had no time to react. 'It's called *positive thinking*,' she said. 'Now, thank you for – ' She stopped, her eyes suddenly wide.

Andy glanced over his shoulder to see what she was looking at. 'What is it?' he asked. 'What's wrong?' Almost directly across the road from where Sandra lived was a narrow alleyway with an arched entrance. She seemed to be staring towards it, but the alley was unlit and he could see nothing there.

Sandra shook her head. 'It's nothing. Thank you for seeing me home, Andy. I think I can manage the rest myself.'

Before he could react, she'd run up the stone steps and was opening the front door. So much for inviting himself in for coffee. Andy turned and walked away, wondering disconsolately what had gone wrong with the evening. When he reached the end of the road he stopped briefly and looked back, half hoping she might still be standing in her doorway.

There was no sign of Sandra, but for just the barest fraction of a second he thought he caught sight of a cloaked figure standing in the shadows near the alleyway. He blinked, half shook his head, and the figure was gone.

Despite his disappointment about Sandra, Andy grinned. A *cloaked* figure! He'd been watching too many Dracula movies.

TWO

Maybe Sandra really was psychic. Andy got the call from Gerald Arnold the very next morning. Not that it was the big break exactly, not a recording contract or anything like that. But Gerald Arnold owned a club.

'Listen, Mr Clarke,' Arnold said in an adenoidal voice that made every word sound like a sneer, 'the question is, can your boys play Saturday?'

'Saturday?' echoed Andy, who wasn't quite awake yet.

'Hey, don't tell me it's short notice,' Arnold said. 'I *know* it's short notice. I had Miller Savage booked this past three months and what do they do to me? They get 'flu. Every one of them except Pete Miller and what good's he on his own? Only told me yesterday – how's that for short notice?'

'Very short, Mr Arnold,' Andy agreed. 'I think we—'

'Today's – what? Thursday? So where am I going to find a top group at a day's notice? Two days, if you count today, which nobody does, of course, even if I ring them in the morning. So I figured, if you can't get a name group, get an up and comer. Somebody mentioned the *Grave Robbers*.'

'*Diggers*,' Andy corrected him.

'Sorry?'

'*Gravediggers*,' Andy said. 'My group is called the *Grave*diggers.'

'Ok, but are you free Saturday?'

Andy considered giving him the run-around about consulting his diary, then thought what the hell. No amount of pretending would make the *Gravediggers* a bigger group than they were. 'We're free, Mr Arnold,' he said.

'And you are a rock group?' Arnold asked. 'My kids like rock. I mean you can slip in a little pop, but it's rock they come to hear.'

'We're a rock group, Mr Arnold,' Andy said. 'Definitely rock.'

'We're on Hope Street – you know us?'

'The Crescent Club, Hope Street,' Andy said. He knew it all right. It was small, but it had a reputation. You played at the Crescent and people started to think you were headed somewhere. So far, the *Gravediggers* had only played pubs, mostly to audiences who were too far out of it to tell the difference between rock and reggae. The Crescent packed in kids who danced and drank Tango and actually *listened* to the music. This might not be the big time, but it was a definite step up.

He realised Arnold was saying something. 'Sorry, Mr Arnold?'

'I said, how does eight sound to you?'

'Eight *hundred*?' Andy asked. It was six hundred more than anything they'd been paid before.

7

'Come on, Mr Clarke,' said Arnold, obviously misunderstanding his tone, 'you may think you're good, you may even *be* good, but you haven't got a name. You're no Miller Savage, know what I mean? It's the name brings in my customers and my customers pay the bills. But I tell you what, I'll make it nine. Last offer. Where else you going to get a booking for Saturday at this late notice?'

'Nine hundred sounds good, Mr Arnold,' Andy said, blinking. That was more than two hundred apiece for one night's work.

'We open at nine,' said Arnold. 'Come round the side door at eight-thirty and you can set up.' He cradled the phone without saying goodbye.

Andy stood stock-still for a moment, then suddenly punched the air. 'Yes!' he shouted in delight and triumph.

THREE

That Saturday, during a break between sets, Andy was sitting at a table in the Crescent Club nursing a Coke and almost feeling like he'd made it. It was still early – a shade past ten – but already the place was packed. It was a young crowd, lively and appreciative; just the sort you needed to build a rock group's reputation. He fantasised about them talking to their friends at school on Monday:

'Hey, have you caught the *Gravediggers* yet? Heard them on Saturday – they're really cool!'

Andy glanced around. Dave and Tim were over by the coffee bar, loading up on caffeine. They were surrounded by teenage girls and he'd noticed earlier they'd been signing autographs. That was more than a good omen, that was a *great* omen, although he noted sourly there was no crowd of teenage girls surrounding *him*. Not that it came as any surprise. Dave had the looks and most girls found Tim sort of cute for some reason. Andy was just the founder/leader of the group, which didn't count. All the same, he wished just once somebody would ask *him* for his autograph.

There had been no sign of Sandra since she'd come off stage.

He found himself thinking about the kiss. Actually he'd been thinking about it quite a lot since Wednesday. There was no doubt she'd kissed him back. No doubt at all. What was in doubt was whether it meant anything.

Andy hadn't had a lot of success with girls. In his early teens he developed a case of acne that made the surface of the moon look like a billiard-ball. It resisted every lotion and cream he put on it, then cleared up of its own accord when he was eighteen. Now, two years later, he was trying to make up for lost time, but he had to admit even without the acne he wasn't exactly Diet Pepsi Time with women. Even his mother told him he should try to cultivate a sense of humour.

So, given his famous sense of humour, did Sandra kiss him for a laugh, or was there maybe something a little more serious behind it? Hadn't she asked him to take things more slowly? And didn't that mean she'd been at least considering the possibility that their relationship might get serious? If she didn't, what was the point of taking it slowly? What was the point of kissing him back at all?

Although, of course, he'd been the one to make the move. He'd been the one who stopped at the street corner and, when she looked at him, wondering why he'd stopped, he was the one who took her shoulders, looked her straight in the eye and kissed her. Which was about the bravest thing he'd ever done.

What was the thing in the cloak? asked a voice in his head.

Andy started. The voice was so unexpected, so

vivid, so ... well, almost scary, it caught him completely by surprise. He hadn't thought about the figure in the cloak at all since Wednesday and now, suddenly, it had switched from being a figure in a cloak to a *thing* in a cloak. Except it wasn't either. One minute it had seemed to be there, the next it was gone, which meant it wasn't a figure or a thing at all, but some freak trick of the light. Wow, he really *had* been watching too many Dracula movies.

Andy realised he was sweating and pretended it was the heat. Put a couple of hundred packed bodies in a club the size of the Crescent and everything got overheated. He took a pull on his Coke and wiped his brow. Some deep little kernel of truth inside him said he wasn't sweating because he was too hot, he was sweating because he was scared. Andy ignored it.

But suppose it really had been a thi— a figure in a cloak? What then?

What then nothing! He should frighten the life out of himself like a little kid because some drunk was staggering home from a fancy dress party? Except it wasn't even a drunk – it was a trick of light and shade.

Maybe he was tired. He just couldn't seem to control what was going on inside his head. Although he knew, he positively *knew*, there had been nothing there, Andy found himself cautiously examining what he had seen, coldly analysing the 'What then?'

The alleyway where he'd seen the figure was almost directly opposite the steps to Sandra's place. Anybody lurking in that dark entrance

11

could see her going in and coming out. The creature – *It was a creature now? Give it a rest, Andy!* – would have seen her with Andy, would have seen the kiss at the end of the street, maybe could even have heard the conversation they had at the bottom of her steps.

He remembered the way Sandra had cut that conversation short, the way her eyes had widened, the way she had run in so abruptly. Had she seen the figure too? But that made no sense. If she'd seen anything, she'd have said so. She'd have told him.

Wouldn't she?

'There you are! I've been looking all over!'

Andy jerked so violently he almost spilled his Coke. He turned to find Sandra sliding into the seat beside him. 'Hey,' she said smiling broadly, 'your nerves are shot. Have you been sprinkling funny-powder in your Coke?'

Andy shook his head. 'Sorry. I think I *am* a bit on edge.' *Because of the thing in the cloak*, his mind whispered. 'I suppose because this is an important gig for us,' he said.

Sandra looked around. 'No worries here – they're a great crowd,' she said. 'They love us.'

Andy's mood lightened at once. 'You think so?'

'Absolutely. Didn't you hear them calling for more when we did "Speed of Night"?'

'They're young,' Andy said. 'They get enthusiastic.' He caught her expression. 'What? What is it?'

'Will you listen to yourself!' Sandra said. 'If

there's any way to play down good news, you'll find it, won't you?'

'No, really, I'm only saying—'

'Well, don't,' Sandra told him. 'Try to accept we're playing something better than a pub for a change and they *like* us. They really *like* us!'

She was gorgeous. She was without a doubt the best-looking, most wonderful girl he'd ever seen. All of which, incredibly, made him nervous. He glanced at his watch. 'Is it time to get back?'

She waved her hand impatiently. 'Not yet. Andy, I want to talk to you.'

Andy blinked at her. 'Yes?' It came out wide-eyed and stupid and he tried to kick himself under the table. What was wrong with him? Why was it just so plain impossible to play it cool around a girl? Especially this girl.

'Andy, what would improve the *Diggers*?'

A record contract and a million quid, Andy thought, but he suspected that wasn't what she was getting at. He watched her without speaking.

'A lead singer?' she prompted. 'Would you say a lead singer?'

'Hey,' Andy said, 'you can sing!' He smiled.

She didn't answer the smile. 'You're sweet, but you're also a liar. You and I both know my voice is nothing special. Besides, we're a rock group. We need a guy up front.'

'Maybe. Maybe not.' Wishy-washy! Now he was sounding wishy-washy! It was a miracle she could bear to carry on this conversation!

'No maybe about it,' Sandra said firmly. 'It's lovely to be playing a club like the Crescent, but

13

if we want to go any further, we need to get a voice up front.'

'Easy said,' said Andy easily.

'But where do we find a lead singer – right?' Sandra asked.

'Something like that.'

She leaned across the table. 'Listen, Andy, I just met a boy and he's fantastic!'

Andy stared at her blankly, not sure what she was telling him. His stomach knotted. 'You've fallen for some fantastic guy?'

'No, no,' she snapped impatiently. 'I'm talking about a *singer*! His name's Aaron Priest. He wants to audition.'

'With us?' Andy asked.

'Of course with us! Why else do you think I'm talking to you?'

'Well, tell him to come to rehearsal next Wedn—'

'I'm talking about tonight,' Sandra said. 'I'm talking about right now.'

It was the first time the *Gravediggers* had played a club, their first really classy gig. The last thing Andy wanted was to screw it up by taking on some star-struck kid. He opened his mouth to refuse.

'Just one number,' Sandra said. 'Try him out for just one number. If you don't like him, that's it.'

Andy looked at her without saying anything.

'Andy,' Sandra said, 'he's had experience!'

So what's he want to sing with a bunch of unknowns for? Andy's inner voice asked sourly. Aloud he said, 'I've never heard of Aaron Priest.'

'He sang a bit in the States. Andy, what have we got to lose?'

'Well, I'm not sure . . .' he said, weakening. His problem was he didn't want to refuse Sandra. He didn't want to refuse her anything.

'You won't regret this,' Sandra said at once. She gestured. 'That's him over there, by the pillar.'

Andy looked. The star-struck kid of his expectation evaporated. The man leaning against the pillar was in his twenties. He was tall and loose with long hair and wide brown eyes. No wonder Sandra wanted to try him out. Somehow he managed to look like a rock singer. He caught the turn of their heads towards him and nodded slightly.

For some reason Andy felt a chill of fear.

FOUR

Dave Anderton made the most fuss. 'You should have consulted us,' he said sourly. 'This isn't your band, Andy, it's *ours*.'

'That's what I'm doing,' Andy told him. 'I'm consulting you now.'

'After it's agreed.'

'No, not after it's agreed, Dave. Sandra asked me to try this clown as a favour and I said I'd put it to you guys.' Which was a lie, but not a big one. If Dave and Tim flatly refused, there was no way anybody could sing with the *Gravediggers*.

'Yeah,' said Tim Pender, obviously not believing him, 'but a new member of the group ... I mean, I like Sandra and all, but she can't dictate to the group.'

'Keep your voice down,' Andy hissed urgently. 'She'll hear you!' Sandra was only a few metres away exchanging pleasantries with one of the Crescent staff.

'She *should* hear us,' Dave put in. 'In fact, we shouldn't be talking about this without her.' He raised his voice. 'Sandra – can you come over here a minute?'

Andy cringed, but when Sandra joined them

16

Dave and Tim were suddenly all charm and sweet reason.

'Oh, well, if it's only a try-out for one number ...' Dave said expansively, even though Andy had explained that to him twice. He smiled at Sandra. 'I'd say we could stand still for that. What do you think, Tim?'

And Tim, irritatingly, said, 'Sure, Sandra, no problemo.'

Except there was a problemo and it wasn't with Dave or Tim. It was with Andy, who was starting to feel just a little bit uncomfortable about Sandra pushing some character she'd just met in the club. Why would she want to do that for a complete stranger? Andy knew the answer, of course. He'd known the answer from the moment he saw Aaron Priest standing cool and sexy by the pillar. Sandra was pushing because she fancied him. What other reason could there be?

But when Aaron Priest walked on stage, even Andy had to admit he looked good. He was wearing a dark shirt that picked up the colour of his eyes and tight leather pants with a broad belt studded with medallions. The outfit bottomed off in high-rise cowboy boots which pushed his height beyond the one metre eighty-five mark. He looked like a visiting American, although the boots were more country-and-western than rock.

Tim started laying down a heavy 2/4 beat even before Priest reached the microphone. Dave picked up on keyboards, then Sandra and finally Andy came in, both on guitar, both goosing the strings to bring up the high hound-dog howling tone that matched the mood of the first number. It sounded good and Andy relaxed a little. If the crowd didn't like Priest, at least they'd notice the *Gravediggers* were still playing like a dream.

Priest reached the microphone, jerked it off its stand, held it to his face and let rip with a drawn-out, howling 'Ohhhhhhh' that stopped conversation dead and even managed to climb all over the metallic howling of the two guitars. Then he hit the song, the oldest of the old rock classics, the one that told you where Priest was living now his baby had left him; 'Heartbreak Hotel'.

It was the sort of number amateurs and oldies picked, not something for the young crowd at the Crescent. Yet somehow it worked. A lot of the kids even stopped dancing to listen. It wasn't so much Priest's voice, although his voice was great. It was his presence, the way he moved, the way he reached out and grabbed you by the throat like a pro and wouldn't let go. The scattering of applause that greeted his appearance turned into squeals, then shouts and finally a burst of screaming appreciation that erupted the moment he finished the number.

There was no hesitation, no consultation. The *Gravediggers* went right into the next one on the list, something a little more musically complex this time, the driving 'Dead Ringer for Love'. Aaron Priest belted it out with an energy that was nothing short of amazing and the kids loved that one as well.

By the third (the Jerry Lee Lewis classic 'Great Balls of Fire') Andy was beginning to face up to something he didn't really want to admit. The crowd at the club were paying much more attention to the *Gravediggers* with Aaron Priest than they'd done without him.

It looked like Priest knew it as well. Halfway into the second number he began to play the crowd and by the fifth he was strutting his stuff like Freddie Mercury. Andy watched with mixed feelings. Priest was good, really good. He had the voice and the moves, but most of all he had the energy and the trick of sending it out to roll across his audience like waves in a storm. The man oozed a raw sex appeal that almost crackled.

Which was all great, except as early as the middle of 'Heartbreak Hotel' Andy had noticed something he didn't like at all. He'd noticed the way Sandra was looking at Aaron Priest. He tried to tell himself everybody was looking at Aaron Priest, but that didn't hack it. Sandra wasn't measuring him up as a singer, wasn't measuring him up as a possible professional colleague. What was in her eyes and on her face said clearly she was interested.

Andy looked at her looking at Priest and something inside him would cheerfully have cut off his guitar hand to have her look at him that way.

The band and Priest went into 'Heart of Stone' to give everybody a rest, lifted the tempo a little with the Mick Jagger hit 'I Can't Get No Satisfaction', then upped the ante yet again with another *Stones* smash, 'Jumpin' Jack Flash'. It was about that time Andy started to wonder who Priest reminded him of. With so much *Stones* material it should have been Jagger, but it wasn't.

Then Priest swung into the *Doors* hit 'The End' and suddenly Andy knew – Jim Morrison, the lead singer of the *Doors*.

The voice was a little different, but he'd obviously developed the same way of moving, the same raunchy sensuality. He even looked like Morrison before he grew the beard and played on the resemblance in the way he dressed.

Jim Morrison is dead, a voice said clearly inside Andy's head, the same voice that had hassled him about the figure in the alleyway. Andy pushed it away again. What was the big deal about a Jim Morrison look-alike? There were plenty of singers who tried to look like Elvis or John Lennon or anybody else they thought might help them get ahead in their career. No reason at all why Aaron Priest shouldn't model himself on Jim Morrison.

But all the same, as he watched Priest striding the stage in his tight leather pants, the voice inside his head kept repeating the obvious: *Jim Morrison is dead. Jim Morrison is dead.*

20

FIVE

Andy Clarke knew he was behaving like a prat. It was now Wednesday, four days since the *Gravediggers* performed in the Crescent Club and he'd done nothing about signing up Aaron Priest. Andy also knew why he was behaving like a prat. The word was jealousy, the old green-eyed monster. He was jealous of Priest's talent, jealous of his singing voice, jealous of the way the audience reacted to him, jealous of his sex appeal and, most of all, jealous of the way Sandra had looked at him while he was performing.

Andy knew all this, but couldn't stop his feelings. So far, he hadn't been able to stop acting on his feelings either. He hadn't seen Priest at the Crescent after the gig finished. He hadn't seen Priest since. Sandra had handed him a piece of paper with Priest's details – probably including his phone number; Andy was sure she'd have his phone number – and Andy hadn't even looked at it. What he'd really done was sulk. He wasn't proud of it, but he knew it.

He also knew he wouldn't be able to keep sulking. Both Dave and Tim had asked about Priest at the regular Monday night rehearsal. Sandra hadn't brought it up directly, but it was quite clear everybody assumed Aaron Priest was the new *Gravediggers* lead.

'He may not want to join,' Andy had muttered in his brand-new dog-in-a-manger role.

'Come on,' Dave told him flatly, 'he got Sandra to ask you for an audition.'

Tim, who was quick to read the runes, must have picked up something in Andy's voice because he phoned twice after the rehearsal. Both times he asked when Andy was going to call Priest. Both times Andy somehow managed to change the subject.

He wondered how long he was going to be able to keep it up. His guess was maybe another three days. The *Gravediggers* wasn't a fully professional band yet. Dave worked days on a building site. Tim was a trainee draughtsman in an architect's office. Sandra was somebody's secretary in a computer company. Andy lived out of a bedsit while he tried to push the group to stardom. But they'd all be together on Saturday as support for a band called *Dropstuff* in a big lounge up on the north side. You didn't have to be Nostradamus to predict Dave, Tim and especially Sandra would want to know why Aaron Priest wasn't with them.

There was a knock on the door of Andy's bedsit. 'Andy, you in there? Some smoothie on the phone for Mike King. That's you, isn't it?'

'Thanks, Stella,' Andy called. Mike King was his stage name, or would have been if anybody ever used it. He opened the door in his pyjamas and smiled sheepishly at his neighbour. 'Didn't give a name, did he?'

22

'What am I – your secretary?' asked Stella. She was a pretty girl with curly blonde hair who worked odd hours as a temp. It was her misfortune that the communal phone was on the wall just outside her flat. She grinned at Andy. 'Get the lead out, baby – it's one of the Power Rangers for sure.'

He followed Stella's pert little bottom up the stairs and lifted the dangling phone as she disappeared into her flat. 'Hello?'

'Mike King?'

'Yes?' He felt a rising bubble of excitement. Anybody asking for Mike King was business, which at the very least meant the possibility of another gig. But something about the voice said this might be more than a support spot at a cruddy lounge. Stella's description was right on the button: a smooth, confident, executive sort of voice, backed by a good education and used to getting what it wanted. A real Power Ranger.

'Is that your real name or a stage-name?'

'Stage name,' Andy said. 'My real name's Andrew Clarke. Who is this?'

'Paul Campbell, Windstorm Records,' the voice said. 'I was wondering if you might be free for lunch?'

SIX

Windstorm Records had an office in Priory
Mews which according to Andy's *A to Z* was off
Langston Street on the south side. It didn't look
much when he reached it – he almost missed the
designer plaque – but the minute he stepped
inside the door his excitement took off like a
space shuttle.

Everything about Windstorm said big-time.
He pushed through a glass door into a reception
area with a cinnamon scent that reminded him of
Sandra's perfume. His feet sank into the sort of
carpet that cost more per square metre than the
Gravediggers made in a night. Three beige leather
armchairs were ranged round a low glass table
scattered with the latest issues of a dozen music
magazines. The expected ones were there – *New
Musical Express* and *Rolling Stone* – but there
were also local publications from France,
Germany and Holland, something called *In
Dublin* which he assumed must be Irish, and a
copy of *Variety* from the States which suggested
Windstorm had broader interests than pop music.

He let his eyes wander across the framed
originals on the walls – trendy modern abstracts
in the coolest of cool blues and greens – and over

to a reception desk manned by Naomi Campbell or at very least the most beautiful black girl Andy had ever seen. She favoured him with a sleepy, friendly smile and said, 'Well, hi.'

Andy swallowed hard. 'Appointment with—' It came out too high, so he coughed and hit it again. 'I have an appointment with Mr Campbell. I'm afraid I'm a bit early.'

The girl twinkled. 'You must be Andrew, or do you prefer Mike?'

'Andy's just fine,' he said. There was music playing softly out of hidden speakers. It sounded like Mozart.

The girl gave him full eye contact and the smile looked as if she wanted to take him to bed and eat him whole. 'Early's OK,' she said. 'Paul's really anxious to see you. Why don't you go on up?' She waved casually towards a lift. 'Second floor. Lois will meet you.'

He rode up in the lift wondering if Lois might be Lois Lane because he was definitely starting to feel like Superman. When the door opened on the second floor she turned out to be a tall redhead with legs that ended somewhere near her ears. 'Hi, Andy,' she said softly. 'Paul wants to see you right away.' She made it sound like a royal command, which in the circumstances maybe it was. He followed her down a corridor that had flock paper on the walls and at least five cut-crystal chandeliers. It had the smell of cinnamon as well.

Paul Campbell was no disappointment at all. He was somewhere in his thirties, maybe even a young forty, dressed casually but trendy. He had a square, ever so slightly fleshy face and the sort of deep-set eyes that made you wonder if he was getting enough sleep. His office was cool: two desks, one with a Power Mac and Zoom 28.8X fax modem by the window, the other, larger, in the middle of the room, with a phone/intercom cum electronic control system that looked straight out of Cape Canaveral. There was one of the new, huge, flat screen black screen television sets in one corner and a full-scale top-of-the-range Pioneer remote amp, CD and tape stack in another. Andy wouldn't have minded betting he had Japanese voice control to draw the curtains and lower the lights.

'This is him, Paul,' Lois said at the door, smiling, and Campbell came round his desk, hand out, beaming like a politician at election time. Andy noticed he wore Gucci shoes.

'Hey, great you could come!' Campbell said, sounding like he really meant it. He gripped Andy's hand, shook it twice, then let it go. 'Grab a pew, my man.' He gestured to an armchair big enough to live in. 'How do you take your java?'

'Black, please,' Andy said. He sat and the chair hugged him like a lover.

'You heard the man, Lois. Two Blue Mountain javas.'

'Coming right up, Boss,' said Lois cheerfully and disappeared.

Campbell perched on the edge of the larger desk so he was looking down on Andy, but somehow his smile made sure it didn't look like a power play. 'Andy,' he said, 'I want to hear all about you.'

26

Andy blinked. 'Pardon?'

'Where you're coming from. Your musical philosophy, when you formed the *Gravediggers*, all that.' He tapped his nose. 'I have my reasons '

Andy's excitement climbed another notch. Since the phone call that morning he'd been trying to hold back on the wild, delicious speculations that were crowding his head and turning his insides to water. Every up-and-coming musician dreamed about a call from a record company, but somehow Andy found it hard to believe it really meant much, even when it happened. Record contracts were for other people, not for him. Except that Paul Campbell, who was obviously top brass at Windstorm – maybe even *the* top brass – wanted to know all about him, all about the *Gravediggers* and that meant a serious interest. Nothing else made sense.

Andy took a deep breath and started to talk, concentrating hard on making it sound sensible, coherent and, above all, cool.

Halfway through, Lois reappeared with coffee in tiny Turkish cups with sticks of cinnamon beside the spoons. Andy began to wonder if Windstorm had shares in a spice company; somebody in the place certainly had a liking for cinnamon.

Andy told Campbell everything he could think of. How he'd formed the group shortly after he left school. How he hustled for gigs. How much the audiences liked them. (A little exaggeration here, but nothing you couldn't put down to good salesmanship.) How he figured the world was ready for a big-scale rock revival and how he hoped the *Gravediggers* might spearhead it since they were concentrating on hard rock to the exclusion, more or less, of everything else. He finished and looked expectantly at Campbell.

Campbell glanced at his watch. 'Table's booked for one,' he said. 'Let's move.'

When Andy found where they were going, he wanted to curl up and die. Campbell had booked the Maciocia, arguably the most trendy restaurant in town and certainly the most expensive. It was so far out of Andy's league he couldn't have found it vith a map and compass.

He sat in Campbell's Porsche, sweating in his distinctly less-than-trendy gear of tee-shirt and jeans, tastefully completed by a pair of battered runners, selected in some lunatic attempt to appear laid-back (*Record companies call me every day*). To make it worse, Judge Dredd – *Judge Dredd*! – was prominently featured on the tee-shirt. He knew as soon as they set foot in the Maciocia that some goon with a dinner jacket and an Italian accent was going to sling him out on the street.

But nobody turned a hair. A dark-eyed woman, who looked in some ways more dangerous than any goon, greeted Campbell by name, actually smiled at Andy, and led them both to a window seat. There were no prices on Andy's menu.

Campbell waited until the dessert to hit him with it. 'I was at the Crescent Saturday,' he said.

Andy tried to take it casually. He nodded, not quite trusting himself to comment.

Campbell leaned forward. 'I want to offer you a recording contract,' he said seriously.

SEVEN

Andy let himself into his bedsit in a daze. He knew it had happened, he remembered it happening, but he still couldn't believe it.

The bedsit was a tip. It had always been a tip, but this was the first time he'd really noticed. The *Gravediggers* were going to sign a contract with Windstorm Records They were going on tour. They were going to make records. They were going to make millions.

It couldn't be happening, but it was happening.

He sat down in his only armchair, the one with the springs poking through to rest on the floor, and tried to imagine what might go wrong. It wasn't that he was pessimistic, more that he was superstitious. If he let himself believe everything was going right, it might immediately start to go wrong. So what could go wrong?

He went over everything Paul Campbell said about the business end and could find no problems with any of it. The terms were on the table, negotiable until they had the agreement of everybody in the group. The draft contract was being drawn up. The money was utterly fantastic.

Andy sat back and closed his eyes. *He smelled of cinnamon*, said the voice in his head.

Andy opened his eyes again. He was getting heartily sick of the voice in his head. He knew it was his own thoughts, of course, the voice of his subconscious maybe, but it had developed an infuriating habit of making him waste time on things that were of no importance whatsoever. A trick of light and shade that looked just a little like a figure in a cloak. And now the smell of cinnamon that ran all through Windstorm Records.

So what was wrong with the smell of cinnamon? Nothing was wrong with the smell of cinnamon! Somebody in Windstorm, maybe even Campbell himself, liked cinnamon, that was all. The girl had brought cinnamon sticks with the coffee, for heaven's sake. There was no reason to make a big deal out of the smell of cinnamon. It wasn't as if it was covering up something...

In a minute, Andy thought, he'd phone the others, tell them the news, accept their congratulations, maybe organise a party. They had to celebrate. They had to dance all night and get drunk as skunks. They had to—

... like the scent of corruption.

Andy stopped short. Covering up the scent of corruption? What on earth had made him think that? He'd never been in a place like Windstorm offices. It was bright. It was fresh. It oozed success and money. What was this about corruption? Nothing Paul Campbell said, nothing anybody said, gave even the slightest hint that Windstorm might be crooked.

Except, deep in his heart, Andy knew it wasn't

that sort of corruption. What had come into his head was the sort of corruption that attacks rotting meat . . .

Or corpses.

31

EIGHT

Dave Anderton wasn't allowed to take calls on the building site but Andy rang him anyway. He told somebody with a broad Dublin accent it was a family emergency and was put through without any problem at all. Dave came on breathless and worried. 'That you, Dad? What's happened?'

'It's not your daddy,' Andy said smugly. 'It's your sugar daddy. We just hit the big time, Dave!'

'Andy? What's happening?'

'Windstorm Records,' Andy said. 'That's what's happening.'

'Never heard of them,' Dave said deflatingly.

'Neither had I,' Andy told him honestly, 'but I just had lunch with their MD at the Maciocia. Cool dude called Paul Campbell, drives a Porsche, Gucci shoes. They have offices off Langston Street, very, very smooth. You could drown in the carpets.'

'Who do they handle?' Dave asked, warming.

'I don't know,' Andy said. He gave a little giggle. 'I got so excited I forgot to ask him. But get this, Dave. He wants the *Diggers* on a five-year contract—'

'What?' Dave exploded, suddenly excited.

Andy felt his first surge of gratification. 'That's just the start. He wants Windstorm to manage us—'

Dave's excitement dropped to zero. 'Is that such a hot idea? I mean the company we're signing with being the ones who manage—'

'I know, that's what I said,' Andy cut him off. 'But listen. He says we get our lawyers—'

'We have lawyers?'

'—or whoever we want to check the contract with Windstorm, make sure it's kosher, but once we've signed, Windstorm takes over the management function because they don't just want us to make an album, they want us to make a *name*!' He was parroting something Campbell had said because he'd been impressed by the turn of phrase.

Dave wasn't quite so impressed, or maybe he missed it because he was still obsessing about lawyers. 'We don't have lawyers, do we, Andy?'

'Dave, will you listen? They want us to make an *album*. They want to sponsor a PR campaign and a tour – you listening to me? – a countrywide concert tour to raise our profile – ' (another of Paul Campbell's phrases) ' – before they release the album. And *when* we release the album, they want a simultaneous release of ... are you listening, Dave? ... our *video*! Extracts from which will be used in our commercials, our television commercials, Dave, scheduled on all the independent channels with the right viewer profile, including MTV. And all this is on top of the PR campaign which Paul says will guarantee – his word – will guarantee exposure in the musical press and MTV itself where it counts!'

'Wow,' was all Dave said.

NINE

Despite his lowly position, Tim Pender had a phone on his desk and his own extension number so Andy got through at once and directly.

'I don't like it,' Tim said when Andy broke the news.

'You don't like it? You don't *like* it?' Andy exploded in amazement. 'What don't you like about it?'

'It's too good,' said Tim seriously. 'I don't see why a big-deal outfit like Windstorm would take all that trouble over a totally unknown group like us.'

Andy leaned against the wall beside Stella Compton's door and pounded his forehead with the heel of his left hand. Then he held out the phone and shook his fist at it. He pulled the instrument back to his ear.

'Listen, Tim, the reason Windstorm is taking all this trouble is we're *good*. You know: G – O – O – D. We're a class act and these people are trained to spot up-and-coming talent.'

'Yeah, but—'

'Oh, come on, Tim, what's the matter with you? You're starting to sound like Dave. This is the chance of a lifetime, our break, our ticket to the big-time and you sit there whinging on about—'

'I'm not whinging on. I hear what you're saying, but I just don't see why they're doing it.'

'They're doing it,' said Andy with forced patience, 'because they have to do it. We may be good, we may be up-and-coming, but we haven't upped and comed. I mean, get real, who's actually heard of us yet? Arnold at the Crescent Club, a few pub owners. We're building a following, but it's local. I mean we're not exactly fighting off the groupies are we?'

'I don't know about you, but I'm certainly not,' Tim said.

'What I'm saying,' Andy told him, wondering why he bothered to call people who could turn a Lottery win into bad news, 'is we need to get known nationally. And after that we need to get known *inter*nationally. We need promotion, we need publicity, we need exposure. We need the fans to know how good we are. They don't know how good we are, they won't buy our album. So Windstorm, who stand to make a lot of money if we deliver a hit album, have to make sure everybody's excited about the *Gravediggers* before the album comes out.'

'Mmm,' said Tim uncertainly.

'The plan is to release a single first, which is less costly than a whole album, and promote that. Paul says—'

'Who's Paul?'

'Paul Campbell. The Windstorm MD. I *told* you,' Andy said impatiently. 'Paul says the trick is to get disc jockeys to play your single and to

plug it. Getting a play isn't too difficult, because
they're always looking for new material, so
unless it's absolute crap they'll play it OK. But
getting them to plug it is something else. They
have to like it, really like it, or else owe a few
favours to the people pushing it.'

'Like to Windstorm?'

'Yes, like to Windstorm. If you get enough
disc jockeys playing a number over and over and
telling people this one is hot, then everybody
starts to buy it. Before you know you're into the
charts.' He took a deep breath. 'Once we get an
entry, anywhere in the top fifty, maybe even the
top one hundred, Paul says he can get us a slot
on *Top of the Pops*.'

At long last it hit home. 'Hey!' Tim exclaimed
admiringly. 'That's cool. That's really cool!'

TEN

Andy's bedsit didn't run to a proper bathroom. He washed and shaved in a shower room ingeniously designed to feel like a cupboard and shared with five other tenants. The door, distinguished by two panes of frosted glass, one pink, one blue – presumably to indicate the unisex nature of the facilities – was just across the landing from the phone. He walked in, stuck his head into the shower cubicle and turned on the cold spray.

He ended up with a damp shirt collar but felt more in control. Windstorm was the biggest thing that ever happened to the *Diggers*, maybe the biggest thing that ever would happen to them. It was the break every group hoped for, worked for, prayed for. No wonder he'd been getting over-excited.

The only really neat thing about the shower room was a full length mirror on one wall and Andy stared into it now. The reflection staring back left a lot to be desired as a hard rock idol groupie mega sex god. He was a little overweight, having a tendency to eat crisps when tense. He had to wear glasses, and though he took them off on stage his eyes looked sunken without them. His hair always managed to hang limply no matter what miracle conditioner he tried. There was still a trace of the acne that had devastated his early teens.

Taken one at a time, these things were fine. He was a lot less overweight than Elton John. His specs were a lot more trendy than the ones John Lennon used to wear. He had far more hair than Phil Collins and his skin was better than Keith Richards'. But when you put them all together, the result was disappointing. Not ugly, not exactly repulsive, but definitely off-key. He couldn't even manage to look cute like the kids in *Supergrass*. One of his old girlfriends once said he had nice hands. However you hacked it, that was a strictly limited compliment.

He pushed a rising depression firmly back into its old black box. Whatever his limitations, he was doing OK. He played guitar well – he knew that. He could also hold his own on keyboards and even, at a pinch, on drums. He had a nice dress sense. He had a lot of energy, a lot of drive, a lot of ambition. Best of all, it had started to pay off. No complaints there. The *Gravediggers* were less than a year old and already they'd been offered a recording contract.

He went back out to the phone, dug more coins from his pocket, and started to dial the number that had been making him nervous. He'd burned up the rest of the afternoon making the calls to Dave and Tim. Now it was growing dark and he was fairly sure she'd he home from work.

The phone rang for a long time.

'Yes?' It was a man's voice.

'May I speak to Sandra, please – Sandra Thurston? It's Andy Clarke.' She had a similar set-up to his own, a pay-phone shared between several flats. It was usually answered by a girl called Gail, but this must be one of the other tenants.

'Hold on.' The voice sounded familiar, but he couldn't quite work out why.

Andy waited. He heard a distant, muted, conversation, then Sandra's voice said, 'Andy? Is that you?'

'It's me and it's news,' Andy said cheerfully. 'We've been offered a recording contract.'

This time, at last, the reaction was everything he could have hoped for. 'Hey, wow, for real? A contract? You putting me on?' Then she giggled. 'No, you're not – you wouldn't dare! Who's it with? What's it for? Are we going to be rich? Is it an album or a single? When do we sign? Have you signed already? Is it a big company? How much are they going to pay us? Come on, Andy, tell me about it!'

'I would if you'd let me get a word in,' Andy grinned. His earlier nervousness had disappeared, making him wonder why he'd been nervous in the first place. He leaned casually against the wall and twirled his finger round the phone cord. 'OK,' he said, 'the company is Windstorm, the man is Mr Campbell and the contract is everything you ever dreamed about!'

What happened in the next five minutes made up double for all the bull Dave and Tim had shovelled down the line. Sandra didn't hesitate at all. She enthusiastically approved of everything Andy told her. She hung on his description of the Windstorm office. She made satisfactory impressed noises when he got to the lunch at the Maciocia. She kept saying *Yes ... Yes ... Yes* as he outlined the details of the contract. Unlike Dave and Tim, she had no hesitations, no objections. When he'd finished, she said the one word he'd most wanted to hear without even realising he'd wanted to hear it. She said, 'Congratulations!'

Andy cradled the phone glowing like a bowl of porridge and feeling just as mushy. The feeling lasted all the way down the stairs and into his untidy bedsit. But as he closed the door, it was already starting to fray round the edges.

He knew why, of course. There was one thing he hadn't told Dave or Tim and certainly hadn't told Sandra. The whole deal with Windstorm was conditional. Paul Campbell wanted the *Gravediggers* all right, but only if 'the guy he saw at the Crescent' was their lead singer. Now Andy had to swallow his pride and go get Aaron Priest.

ELEVEN

His wallet was full of rubbish, but he found the paper since he never threw anything away. He unfolded it carefully. Priest's name and address winked up at him in Sandra's neat handwriting, but there was no phone number. For a moment he thought of ringing Sandra back and asking her if she had one, then glanced back at the paper, calculated how far Priest lived from the bedsit and decided to pay a personal call.

It proved to be a big mistake. Aaron Priest lived in what had to be the roughest, sleaziest, most intimidating part of town. At high noon on a sunny day it would have been terrifying to walk through without a police escort. Now, after dark, Andy wouldn't have felt secure if he'd been accompanied by the entire Paratroop Regiment. On top of which, it was still raining.

According to the *A to Z*, you reached the address on Sandra's slip of paper via King Street, Bridge Street and French Church Street. Andy knew King Street by reputation. It was, apparently, home to a teenage street gang known as the Bloods, or the Hoods or the Fangs or some such sinister nonsense. At the beginning of the month, the Bloods had gone on the rampage in reaction to an intrusion by another street gang called the Ghouls (Andy remembered that one perfectly for some reason). By the time the police arrived, the Bloods had broken every window in the street, looted an off-licence, beaten up an elderly pawnbroker and left three of the Ghouls in a critical condition due to stab wounds.

Even now, three weeks later, the signs of the trouble were still evident in King Street. Several windows were boarded, some of them protected only by cardboard. Three dingy shops showed signs of fire damage. A two-way traffic sign creaked and swung in the gusting wind, now held to its pole by no more than a single screw. Nearly half of the streetlamps were broken, leaving the whole area gloomy in the pouring rain.

Fortunately there was no sign whatsoever of the Bloods or whatever they were called, who might have been kept indoors by the rain or might all have been arrested, for all Andy knew. Whatever the reason, he was glad of their absence. Physical violence terrified him. He'd never been in a fight in his life, not even as a child.

He left King Street with a sigh of relief, only to find Bridge Street was even worse. It was a long, empty thoroughfare, wider than King Street and largely featureless. One side comprised crumbling Georgian buildings with faded gold lettering on their windows indicating office conversions for firms that could afford no better. The other side was largely hidden by an endless length of builder's screening covered in ornate graffiti. Beyond it, half demolished buildings stood against the rain-swept sky like broken teeth. Most of the road was up and a diversion was in place, which explained why the street was so empty. A prominent notice by a row of cones stated blandly:

THIS WORK IS NECESSARY FOR THE IMPROVEMENT OF YOUR CIVIC AMENITIES. WE HOPE YOU WILL UNDERSTAND AND FORGIVE SUCH INCONVENIENCE AS MAY BE CAUSED.

Somebody had scrawled a terse two-word response across it in spray paint. Andy grinned despite his nerves.

The grin disappeared when he found that the entrance to French Church Street – where Priest lived according to Sandra – was through an archway and along an alley with no streetlights whatsoever. Andy turned up his coat collar and plunged down it with all the enthusiasm of a kamikaze conscript. Although he emerged – safely – only moments later, his heart was pounding so fiercely he actually had to stop to catch his breath.

French Church Street stretched before him like a remnant of another age. There was a lit and noisy public house (*The Cat and Canary*) halfway down, but otherwise the buildings were largely in darkness. The roadway was half cobbled, an arrangement that must have been murder on motorists. The houses looked Victorian and seemed in worse repair than those being knocked down in Bridge Street. To judge by the lack of lights, most of them were derelict. What was Aaron Priest doing in a district like this? More to the point, *where* was Aaron Priest living in a district like this?

Andy stopped under a streetlight and consulted his scrap of paper. The address was National Towers, which had to be the high-rise block which stood like a *Blade Runner* remnant at the far end of the street.

Andy approached it with trepidation. The entrance to National Towers was illuminated by a single bulb protected by a strong wire screen. When the block was built, you pushed through double doors. Now only one of them was left and even that was hanging from a hinge.

The entrance hall was covered in obscene graffiti. There was a lift directly facing him and concrete stairs to his right. He walked quickly to the lift and pressed the button. Lights blinked above the door, but part of the panel had been torn away, revealing twisted wires. He pressed the button again as fear made him impatient.

'Don't work.'

Andy jumped, but when he looked round it was no more than a rheumy old lady shuffling down the corridor beside the stairs.

'The light came on,' Andy said to her receding back.

She shrugged without even bothering to look round. If he was fool enough to stand beside a broken lift all night that was nothing to her. Andy glanced back at the winking lights, then decided to believe her. Priest was only on the third floor. It wouldn't kill him to use the stairs.

45

A part of his mind whispered reassuringly that if a rheumy old lady, who looked well over seventy, could survive in these flats, a fit young man like himself was certainly in no danger.

A lot of the reassurance disappeared when he actually reached the third floor. He could hear voices even before he emerged from the stairwell and as he pushed into the corridor he saw a group of skinheads had clustered around the door to one of the flats. They had their backs to him and were hunched over as if concentrating intently on something. He guessed a drug deal might be going down.

Andy was painfully aware the sudden pounding of his heart was not entirely due to the long climb. If he turned right, he would have to push past the skinheads. One of them, he noticed, had a swastika tattooed on his scalp.

He checked the numbers on the nearest flats and gave a silent sigh of relief. It looked as though Priest's pad was somewhere further down to his left. He moved into the corridor as unobtrusively as possible and walked quietly away from the skinheads, fervently praying they would not look up. They didn't, and in a minute he had turned a corner. Andy forced himself to calm down. There was always the problem of getting out, of course, but he'd worry about that when the time came.

He began to move slowly down the corridor checking the doors. Some of them had numbers, but there was a definite problem in that most of them did not. All of them had chips gouged out.

Despite the missing numbers, he worked out the system eventually and deduced where to find

46

Priest's door. It was one of those without a number and as he approached it he discovered it was also one of those without a bell. There was a small hole in the wall which, he assumed, had once housed a bell-push, but there was not even a trace of wiring now. He reached up and knocked gently. What was Aanon Priest doing in a pit like this?

He knocked again, louder this time.

'What do you want, Sunshine? You looking to score?'

Andy jerked round to discover his worst fears had materialised behind him. The skinhead with the swastika tattoo was glaring at him. He had a Glaswegian accent which somehow went well with the studded leather waistcoat.

Andy tried a weak grin. 'Nothing like that. I'm looking for a friend.'

The skinhead failed to grin back. 'Then you're looking in the wrong place, Sunshine.' He jerked his head. 'That door you're knocking on is mine.'

Andy stepped back as if the door had bitten him. 'Sorry. Wrong door. Sorry. I just—' He moved his hands stupidly. Swastika Scalp's companions came round the corner in a group and stared. They had curiously vacant, malignant expressions.

'Now the thing is, Sunshine,' Swastika Scalp said smoothly, 'sometimes the police—' he pronounced it 'poliss' ' – send wee fellas round to my place pretending they're after a score, on account the pigs think I might be dealing. You wouldn't be one of them wee fellas, would you?'

Somehow Andy kept the grin plastered in

place. 'No, nothing like that,' he said. He tried to edge away from the door. Why, in the name of God, had he not come this morning, in daylight, while these thugs were probably in bed sleeping off the night before?

'I thought you'd say that, Jimmy.' The change from 'Sunshine' sounded weirdly ominous. 'But the thing is, you'd say that anyway.'

Andy looked from Swastika Scalp to his blank-faced mates and back again. He knew he was in trouble, but just how much trouble would depend on how he acted in the next few minutes. His whole instinct prompted him to run, to try to push past these louts and make a break for the stairs. Either that or beg, preferably on his knees. But he had the feeling neither was a particularly good plan, despite his instinct.

'Wouldn't you?'

'Wouldn't I what?' asked Andy.

'Say that anyway.' Swastika Scalp took a step forward and pushed his face close to Andy's own.

Without thought, Andy did the bravest thing of his life. He reached out, placed the flat of his hand on Swastika Scalp's chest and pushed. The skinhead fell back a pace, possibly more from surprise than the force of the shove. 'Listen,' Andy hissed, dropping the idiot grin, 'I'm not police. I'm not here to buy drugs. I'm not trying to get mixed up in your stupid little games. I'm here to find a friend of mine called Aaron Priest ... Sunshine.'

He more than half expected a concerted attack. Instead, Swastika Scalp took another step backwards and glanced at his companions. Their expressions had become wary.

Swastika Scalp looked back at Andy. 'The Yank?' he asked.

'That's him,' Andy nodded, trying to look tough. He had the distinct feeling some invisible advantage had just swung in his direction, although he couldn't figure out what or why.

Swastika Scalp jerked his head. 'That's his door over there.' He stared at Andy for a moment, then nodded to his friends. To Andy's astonishment they drew back, then moved off down the corridor. None of them looked back.

Andy watched them until they disappeared from sight round the corner, then walked to the door Swastika Scalp had indicated. He hesitated. There was something oddly disturbing about the whole incident – and not just the fright he'd felt when he was being threatened. It took him a moment to work out what it was. Then it hit him. It was the expression on the skinheads' faces when he mentioned Aaron Priest.

It was difficult to believe, yet he was certain of what he had seen. Every one of them had been afraid.

TWELVE

Priest's door had no bell either. Andy knocked and froze as it swung open a crack. The door was unlocked and unlatched! He could hardly believe it. Who left their door open in a place like this?

Somebody who frightens people, whispered the voice in his head. *Somebody who frightens people so much he knows they won't dare come in!*

Andy brushed the voice aside. He'd reached the stage where his nerves were so much on edge he was likely to imagine anything. Threats where there were no threats. Fear on the faces of thugs. He reached up and knocked again, more forcefully. The door swung open far enough for him to see two things. The first was that the lock was not broken. The second was that there was no light inside.

What to do? He didn't know Priest well enough to barge into his flat, even if the door was left open. But it was still important that he contacted the man somehow. And soon. If he didn't, he could never explain it to Sandra. And without Priest there'd be no Windstorm contract.

Andy pushed the door a little wider and called, 'Anybody home?'

If Aaron Priest really was out, he couldn't have

gone far. Nobody in their right mind would leave their place unattended for long in a neighbour-hood like this. Even if he did frighten people a little.

'Aaron? You in there? Anybody home?'

There was no sound from inside. In fact he suddenly realised how quiet everything had become. His voice echoed. His knock had sounded loud in the silence. It felt as if the whole building was holding its breath, waiting.

Andy shrugged. What had he been telling himself about nerves and imagination? This was really getting out of hand.

'Aaron? Aaron Priest? It's Andy Clarke – can I come in?'

Did he want to go in? Did he really want to go in? He pushed that question aside as well. Of course he really wanted to go in. He really wanted to talk to Aaron Priest. He really wanted the guy in his band. Maybe there would be a few problems with Sandra. Maybe Andy would have to swallow his pride about who was going to be the *Gravediggers'* star. But Priest would have his compensations. The Windstorm contract was worth a fortune to them all. They were heading for the big-time. Taking on Priest was a small enough price to pay for that.

He stuck his head around the door. There was a curious, musty smell inside, as if something had died and just begun to rot.

'Aaron? Anybody home?'

He pushed the door wide. Light from the corridor showed a smallish hallway. A shoddy grey-brown carpet on the floor was actually worn through to concrete just inside the door. A crushed beer-can lay in one corner, otherwise the hall was empty.

Andy licked his lips, glanced briefly behind him, then stepped inside. The musty, dead smell grew a little stronger.

'Hello? Hello?'

There were three doors leading off the hallway. No light shone under any of them. Andy took a troubled step forward and his foot crunched on something that sounded like broken glass.

'Hey, Aaron!'

He was astonished how nervous he felt. What was the worst that could happen? Priest had gone out for a pack of cigarettes or a pint of milk and came back to find Andy in his hallway. Big deal. Andy hadn't broken in, hadn't come to steal the family silver. He was the bearer of glad tidings, for heaven's sake! Aaron Priest (who asked for the audition, remember), would fall on his neck like . . .

. . . *a vampire* . . .

. . . a long-lost brother, would welcome him with open arms. He had nothing, absolutely nothing, to worry about.

Behind him, the door slammed shut.

THIRTEEN

Andy only just managed to stifle a scream. With the door shut, he was in pitch darkness. He stepped back, fumbled, tried to open it. With mounting panic, he discovered it was jammed, or locked. He found the handle, twisted, pulled, rattled, his breath coming in tight gasps. He was trapped! Something had crept in to close the door and he was trapped!

After a moment that came close to utter panic, he forced himself to be calm. This was ridiculous. Of course he wasn't trapped. The door had blown closed in a draught of wind, that was all. These old Fifties tower blocks were full of draughts. The door had probably clicked on a latch. If he could see what he was doing, he could have it open in a minute.

For the first time in his life, Andy Clarke regretted he was not a smoker. If he'd been a smoker, he would be carrying a lighter or matches. As it was, he was carrying nothing that could make a light. He promised himself if he ever got out of this nerve-wracking place, he would never go anywhere again without a box of matches.

It occurred to him that the panic hadn't really gone away. Inside his head, he was still racing round like a hamster on a tread mill. He didn't need matches. There was bound to be a light switch somewhere, probably beside the door.

The dead smell seemed to be growing stronger. He thought it might just be the result of standing in the dark. Your senses sharpened in the dark.

He ran his hand over the wall at shoulder height. The surface texture felt powdery, like that of an unfinished building. Eventually he found the switch. His fingers told him it was the old-fashioned brass-bound type with a protruding knob, not the modern plastic flip-flop. He pushed it into the ON position with a satisfying click, but nothing happened.

Andy flicked the switch twice more without result. The panic was growing again like some mutated fungus and he fought it back savagely. There had to be another switch somewhere. Cautiously he began to move around the walls, carefully feeling them with his hands, desperately searching.

He came to one of the doors without having found a switch. A fumbling hand reached a plastic knob. He turned it, wondering if he should have knocked.

Knocked? Any fool could tell this flat was empty. Empty and silent.

He pushed the door, which swung open easily.

The room inside had a window so that it was eerily illuminated by the dim glow of the street-lights outside. There was a light switch immediately inside the door, but it proved as useless as the one in the hall. Andy stood straining his eyes, willing them to adjust to the light.

A truly awful thought occurred to him. Maybe this wasn't Priest's flat! He'd only the word of Swastika Scalp to go on after all, not the most obviously trustworthy of sources. Suppose the lout had decided to have a little fun? Suppose he'd sent him to this door precisely because he knew it was open and that Andy would probably go in. Suppose he then put through an anonymous call to the police: 'Break in at National Towers, Officer. Better hurry...'

Andy pushed that one out of his mind. He seemed to be doing nothing but push thoughts out of his mind since he set foot in this damn building. He looked around in the half-light. The room seemed to be a bedroom. At least it had a bed in it. But there was almost nothing else. No chairs, no wardrobes, no dressing-table, no chest of drawers, no table, not even a lamp. A tall box was silhouetted beside the bed, maybe a filing cabinet, maybe some sort of upright cupboard, maybe even...

... *an upright coffin* ...

... a blanket chest, although the proportions were all wrong for a blanket chest.

There weren't even curtains on the window. What sort of man had a bedroom without curtains on the window? And why wouldn't the damn lights work! He flicked the switch again in frustration.

Andy took a step into the room and at once something shook itself into life near the bed. He started violently and only just managed to stop himself hurtling back out into the tiny, dark hallway. A gentle humming sound filled the air, strangely familiar.

55

Cautiously Andy took another step forward The humming seemed to be coming from the box beside the bed. What was going on? What sort of lunatic was Aaron Priest? What sort of weird machine did he have beside his bed?

Another step and suddenly, out of nowhere, Andy recognised the sound. He felt relief flood over him. Moving with new-found confidence he walked across to the box. Close up he found exactly what he expected. It was a fridge! An odd place to keep it, but it was definitely a fridge.

Andy tugged at the door and suddenly the area by the bed was flooded with light as a blast of cold air hit him. He peered inside, half expecting cans of beer or a few midnight snacks, although a dark side of him whispered there might just be packs of white powder. But the only thing inside was a shallow tray of . . .

Andy frowned. Of what? It looked like a seed tray full of earth. Except you didn't put seeds in a fridge. They needed heat, not cold.

He left the door open and looked round the room. Nothing new sprang out of the shadows in the extra light. The room had a bed and an almost empty fridge and that was that. Not even a picture on the walls. Not even Home Sweet Home in poker work.

There was fungus growing on the bed. Andy stared at it in disgust. The mould had spread in an uneasy stain across the top of the mattress. There were no blankets, no sheets, no pillows, just a rickety frame and a mattress covered in mould. This was a bed that nobody slept in, a bed that nobody had slept in for months, or even years.

He decided to leave the fridge open. He doubted it would hurt anything Priest was doing with the soil tray and it was reassuring to have more light. As he moved back towards the bedroom door, a thought struck him. Part of his mind had assumed the reason why the light switches didn't work was that Priest maybe hadn't paid his electricity bill. If he lived in this sort of squalor, maybe he was simply broke. But now it was clear the electricity hadn't been cut off. Priest simply lived in a place that didn't have lights. It had a bed that no one slept in. It had a fridge that kept soil cool but held not a scrap of food, not so much as a carton of milk. He was finding it difficult to imagine anybody living in a place like this.

Anybody human.

Andy pushed the thought viciously aside and moved back into the hallway, now illuminated by the spillover light from the window and the fridge in the bedroom. He was certain the flat was empty. Priest might return soon, but he certainly wasn't here now.

In the hallway, Andy looked back at the front door. Now his eyes had adjusted the extra light let him see that his earlier panic was ridiculous. The door had closed on a Yale lock, but there was no problem at all opening it from the inside. He was not trapped, not trapped at all.

With the relief came a brilliant idea. He would leave Priest a note! All he had to do was scribble a few words asking Priest to ring him urgently, maybe even hinting at the recording contract. It was so simple, so obvious, he was astonished he hadn't thought of it before. He searched his pocket, found a pen at once, but not a single scrap of paper. Damn! Not so much as an old bus ticket.

But he wasn't about to give up on a great idea just yet. Especially when the alternative was to hang around this nightmare place and wait for Priest. All he had to do was find paper, any paper. Once he wrote the note, he could leave it in the hallway and get out. Priest needn't even know he'd been in the flat – he could have posted it through the letterbox, or pushed it under the door. Just one small scrap of paper was his ticket out of here.

He opened one of the two remaining doors and struck gold at once. He was in a bathroom. This one had a window as well, high up on the wall, with blue frosted glass. There was some sort of light – presumably a street lamp – almost directly outside, so the illumination was even better than the bedroom. Andy moved straight for the loo. Loo paper wasn't ideal for a note, but it was better than nothing.

Except there was no loo paper. No furniture in the bedroom, no food or drink in the fridge and now no paper in the loo. He searched for a few moments to make sure he hadn't overlooked a roll pushed behind the bowl or somewhere, then admitted defeat.

But he wasn't beaten yet. Maybe Priest had something in his living-room that would do. Andy shut the bathroom door and opened the last remaining door off the little hallway. He'd seen the bedroom and the bathroom, so he calculated this had to be the living-room. From everything else he'd seen, it would be spartan, maybe just a table and chairs with something to cook on. Nothing fancy, but there would be – there were bound to be – a few personal bits and pieces left by Priest. Among them, think positive, would be a piece of paper.

Andy froze. Streetlights illuminated this room as well and his eyes had adjusted enough for him to see quite easily. There was no table, no chairs, no cooker.

Just a large, bare room with a coffin in the middle of the floor.

FOURTEEN

The *Gravediggers* met each Tuesday and Thursday in *Make Mine Music*, a dingy but professionally equipped set of rehearsal rooms on the east side, close to where Tim Pender was still living with his parents. The ghastly name was the brainchild of the rooms' owner, a Pakistani called Abayakhan Abud. It was a running gag that the first band member there would greet the others with the words 'Welcome to my humble Abud!'

Andy was first in the rooms on Thursday, but when Dave arrived, joking was the last thing on his mind. 'We have trouble, Dave,' he said.

'It's the contract, isn't it?' Dave asked at once. He turned to strike the wall with the side of his fist. 'I knew it! I bloody knew it! Andy, that was always too good to be true. I mean, we're –'

'No, not the contract,' Andy cut him short. 'I mean it is, but not—' He shrugged as if a great weight had settled on his shoulders. 'Listen, I need to talk to you. And the others.'

'The others aren't here yet. Talk to me.'

'It's Priest,' Andy said.

'What about him?' The panic in Dave's eyes lifted another notch. 'He's turned us down! I knew he would!'

'Of course you didn't know he would,' Andy said irritated. 'Will you list—'

But Dave hardly seemed to hear him. 'He's heard about Windstorm. Bet you anything. Bet you a million pounds. He heard about Windstorm and now he's gone to make his own deal with them. That's what happened, didn't it?'

'Dave—'

'You didn't tell him, did you? I mean about Windstorm? You didn't tell him before we had him signed up? Andy, say you didn't tell him! Not even you could be—'

'Cripes, Dave, will you shut up? I didn't tell Priest anything. I haven't even *seen* him. I—'

'Not seen him? You were supposed to sign him up! That was the whole point. Windstorm won't—'

Andy, who had never been in a fight in his life, said, 'Dave, one more word and I will smash you in the mouth, I swear.' He glared. Dave looked startled, but subsided. Andy said, 'Now, will you listen?'

'I'm listening! I'm listening! Speak to me!'

'I went to Priest's place, but he wasn't there. He isn't on the phone. Or at least if he is, I don't have a number. The place is a nightmare, but that doesn't matter.' He stopped. He'd rehearsed how to say this over and over, but now the moment had come, he didn't know how to say it at all. Dave stared at him expectantly. Eventually Andy said, 'Aaron Priest is a vampire.'

Dave hlinked. 'Pardon?'

Andy rubbed his eyes. 'Listen, I know how this must sound, but—'

'What's your evidence?' Dave asked.

'I'm sorry?' Andy asked.

'I mean, I believe in vampires,' Dave said seriously, 'but how do you know he is one?'

'You believe in vampires?' Andy, who had gone through agonies wondering how he was going to convince the others, now found his mind had done a somersault. He couldn't accept that Dave was serious.

'I'm not stupid,' Dave said. 'There's a lot of evidence. *Interview With The Vampire* wasn't really fiction, you know. Anne Rice just pretended it was because nobody would believe the truth. But they're rare. I mean they're *really* rare. I'd need a lot of convincing that you'd found one in the cellar.' He looked at Andy.

'You want to know why I think Aaron Priest is one?'

Dave nodded.

It was too easy. He'd expected disbelief, ridicule. Cautiously he said, 'It's his flat. If you can call it a flat. It's the creepiest place you've ever seen. I mean, seriously creepy. No furniture, no food. The bed hasn't been slept in for months. He keeps a tray of soil in his fridge and a coffin in his living-room!'

'How do you know?' Dave asked.

'How do I know? I was *there*! I was right there in his living-room!'

'I thought you said he wasn't home when you called.'

Puzzled, Andy said, 'He wasn't.'

'Then how did you get into his living-room?'

'The door was open. I mean, the door of his pad was open.'

Dave stared at him. 'You went into his place when he wasn't there? That's trespassing, man!'

'What's the matter with you, Dave? Are you deaf or just plain stupid? I'm telling you this guy is a vampire and you're hassling me about *trespassing*? Come on!'

'I take it this means you didn't sign him up with the group,' Dave said seriously.

FIFTEEN

Tim bustled in, wrestling with an amp and carrying his drumsticks in his teeth. He set the amp down gratefully, removed the drumsticks and said, 'We need a place on the ground floor. Those stairs are going to kill me.'

'Come over here, Tim, listen to this,' Dave said. 'Go on, Andy, tell him what you just told me.'

Andy went over his story again, playing down the trespass angle. When he hit the punch line, Tim said, 'I don't believe in vampires.'

'Hey, like, maybe—' Dave put in cautiously.

But Tim cut him off. 'But even if I did, Andy, you saw nothing at all that proves he's one.'

Andy blinked. 'Nothing? You call a coffin in the living-room *nothing*?'

Tim actually smiled. 'I had a great-aunt who slept in a coffin for the last three years of her life. Said she wanted to make sure it was comfortable before she went. She wasn't a vampire – just eccentric.'

'What about the soil in the fridge?' Andy asked fiercely.

'Yeah, native soil and all that,' Dave said, rowing in on Andy's side. Apparently his convictions about vampires forced him to defend them against an unbeliever.

'They're supposed to sleep on native soil,' Tim said patiently. He turned to Andy. 'Did you see any soil in the coffin?'

Andy stared at him. He hadn't looked in the coffin. He'd seen it and run from Priest's flat like a bat out of hell. Eventually he said, 'Why would he keep soil in the fridge?'

'Seeds,' Tim said irritatingly. 'It was just a seed tray.'

'You propagate seeds in the warm, not the cold,' Andy said firmly, echoing an earlier thought.

'Not all of them. Some of them you have to keep in the cold for a while. Mimics hibernating conditions.'

'There was no food in the place!' Andy snapped, his fear and frustration pushing him towards outright anger. 'Nothing. What do you think he lives on?'

'Well, not blood, that's for sure,' Tim told him. He shrugged elaborately. 'So he's run out of milk? So he hasn't done the shopping? So he lives like a pig? That only proves he's a slob, not a vampire.'

Dave, despite his belief in vampires, said, 'Maybe he's got something there, Andy. I mean, we can't bad-mouth this fellow too much – we need him in the group.'

Before Andy could comment, Tim said, 'Know what I think happened?'

'What?' Andy asked sourly.

'No offence, Andy, but I think you got

spooked. I think you went into this dark pad in this grotty building and, hey, you're an imaginative type. You started to put two and two together and ended up making five.'

There was something in that. The place *had* scared him. It had scared him a lot. When he finally saw the coffin, all he'd wanted to do was turn and run out of the flat, out of the building, out of the street. Frankly, all he'd wanted to do was run and keep running until he was home with the door locked. Was it possible Tim was right?

Andy already knew he didn't really want Aaron Priest in the group, not really. He wanted the Windstorm contract, wanted the money, wanted the fame, but would very much have preferred that Priest wasn't part of it. But that was nothing to do with vampires. That was to do with the fact he was jealous of Priest, jealous of the way Sandra looked at him. Was it possible he'd let his jealousy run away with him to the extent he'd convinced himself Priest was a vampire? Dammit, until he walked into Priest's flat, Andy hadn't even known he believed in vampires.

'Andy! Tried to phone you earlier! I owe you a huge apology!'

Andy turned and his stomach knotted. Behind Sandra, Aaron Priest pushed through the door of *Make Mine Music* looking like the sex symbol of the twenty-first century in his leather pants, black shirt and cowboy boots. He raised one hand in a laid-back greeting.

Andy glanced quickly at Dave, but before

either of them could say anything, Sandra was running across to hug Andy. 'I really am so sorry,' she said. 'You must think I'm a complete idiot!'

She released Andy and beamed at him. 'Still, all's well that end's well,' she said. 'I know it's not my place and you're leader of the group but I had to make amends and I was sure you wouldn't mind.'

Andy stared at her, wondering what on earth she was talking about. Despite her brittle energy, she looked pale and drained.

Sandra said, 'You don't know what I'm talking about, do you?'

Andy shook his head. Out of the corner of his eye he noticed Dave moving warily away from Aaron Priest.

'You went to see Aaron, didn't you?'

Andy nodded. 'Yes.'

'Somebody told him you'd been asking for him. But you didn't find him, did you?'

'Well, he wasn't . . . home,' Andy said. Maybe Aaron Priest wasn't a vampire – looking at him now in his leather pants and cowboy the idea seemed ridiculous – but he still made Andy nervous.

'No, of course he wasn't home,' Sandra said. 'And that was all my fault.'

All her fault? Had Priest been with her when Andy called at his flat? All of a sudden he remembered the male voice that answered when he'd called Sandra to tell her the news about Windstorm. It had sounded familiar then. Was it Priest's voice?

'Ah, Sandra . . .' Dave began hesitantly.

But Sandra wasn't listening. She was looking intently at Andy. 'That's why I owe you an apology,' she said.

Andy blinked. He just couldn't get his head together when she looked at him, not even slightly, not when her eyes did something deep inside him that set all sorts of hormones marching. 'You do?' he asked stupidly.

'I gave you the wrong address,' she said. 'No wonder you couldn't find Aaron. I sent you to the wrong flat.'

SIXTEEN

Aaron Priest joined the *Gravediggers* with smiles all round. (Nobody mentioned that hilarious misunderstanding about vampires. Even Dave showed uncharacteristic tact.) The Windstorm contract got signed in Campbell's office late one evening to an accompaniment of champagne flutes. Paul Campbell talked about the future. Everybody was blissfully, deliriously happy.

Except maybe Andy.

Less than a week after the signing, he was standing in a drizzling rain in front of an address Campbell had given him and feeling just the smallest bit disappointed. The street was OK: a row of well-kept Georgian buildings converted into offices. But Gemini Studios were so tiny that even with the address in his hand Andy nearly missed it. They didn't even rate the ground floor, but were located in a basement so you had to rattle down a metal staircase to reach them. The plaque said:

> GEMINI

which was a bit more creative than *Make Mine*

Music, but not much. Another sign, handwritten, said:

The bell's over there →

Andy found the bell and pressed it. He started thinking of Sandra, something that was becoming a habit these days. He'd asked her out three times since they'd signed the contract. Each time she refused – nicely, politely, gently, but refused. There was always something else she'd promised to do. He had no reason to believe she was telling him lies, but he believed she was telling him lies. Face it, he was thinking of Sandra and Aaron Priest. Andy was sure she was seeing him.

He was also worried that she was sick. Her colour was awful and she was developing dark rings around her eyes. When she played, she'd taken to wearing heavy make-up. Yet she always insisted she was feeling fine and certainly showed no loss of energy. A part of him wondered if she might be doing drugs. Another, even more suspicious part, wondered if she might be doing drugs supplied by Aaron Priest. The thought chilled him.

He pressed the bell again. After a while the door was opened by a painfully thin youth who looked stoned. He smiled benignly and said, 'Hi.'

'Andy Clarke,' Andy said. There was no change in the youth's expression so he added, 'Mike King.' He wondered suddenly why he'd ever bothered with a stage name. All it did was make him feel schizophrenic.

The youth smiled like an angel. 'Why didn't you say, man?'

It was Andy's first time inside a recording studio and he was astonished how cramped it was. Just inside the door he found himself in a minuscule hallway cluttered with, of all things, cleaning buckets and brooms. It was here the youth decided to introduce himself – 'Like, I'm Sidney, man,' – and they stood nearly shoulder to shoulder trying to shake hands.

From the broom cupboard they squeezed into a hall with whitewashed walls and a single upright chair for visitors. Gemini wasn't owned by Windstorm. Paul Campbell explained it was far more economical for the company to hire independent studios as they needed them rather than sink money into equipping their own.

A plump, cheerful character in his early thirties was adding his feet to the clutter on the reception desk. He smiled at Andy in a friendly fashion as Sidney explained, 'This is Sandy King, Pete. He's in the session with Sammy.'

Pete, who had a girlie magazine on his lap, jerked a thumb vaguely behind him. 'Show him the way, Sid!' His tone suggested they'd been having trouble with Sid's brain.

'Oh, yeah, right,' Sidney said.

They had to push past the desk to get into a narrow corridor. Andy noticed the doors along it were the sliding variety, presumably because there was no space for them to open outwards. Some of them were pulled back and he could see there was no space to open inwards either. The rooms were almost filled to capacity with metal frame shelving jam-packed with tapes and CDs.

Sidney led him into a control booth which overlooked the studio through a glass wall. Two beanpole engineers, introduced as Martin and John, were eating sandwiches. Through the wall, Andy could see the *Gravediggers* gathered round a balding middle-aged man in a crumpled suit. They looked for all the world like ball-players getting a pep talk from their coach before a game.

He passed a few words with the hungry engineers before Sidney pointed him towards the door to the studio. As he pushed through, he discovered it was a double-door set-up, like the airlock of a spaceship, with whispering rubber sealing, presumably to keep everything soundproof. As he opened the second door, Dave looked round and sang out, 'Hey, here's the late Mr Clarke!'

Then the balding middle-aged man was bustling across to introduce himself as Sammy Walling, the producer, and suddenly, looking round the studio with its amps and its mikes and its gear and its snaking cables, a studio maybe a million times larger than any of the poky rooms in the Gemini offices, a studio that was clean and smelled of electronics and plastic, a studio that had real carpet on the floor, looking round all this Andy felt a surge. The *Gravediggers*' first single! They'd arrived!

SEVENTEEN

The surge didn't last.

'Good to meet you, kid,' Sammy Walling said, pumping his hand. 'Listen, I don't want to rush you, but time is money, so I thought now you're here we'd get started right off.'

'Yes, fine,' Andy said. 'What do you want me to do?'

'Just get up there by your mike. The music's on the stands. I've talked to the others – everybody knows where it's at. We'll do a run-through for levels, help settle everybody down as well, then if it's OK, I'll give you the sign and we'll do it for real. I'll be in the box. You want to talk to me, just talk – there's always a feed from studio to box, even when the red light's off. Any questions?'

'What happens if we fluff it?' Andy asked anxiously.

Sammy Walling shrugged. 'You fluff it, you fluff it. Small fluffs we can fuzz. Major fluffs, we do a retake. No big deal either way. Chances are we'll have to do it a few times anyway. Nobody ever gets it right first time.'

'Yes, OK.'

'Don't worry – you'll be great.' Sammy

grinned suddenly. 'And if you aren't, we can always play around with the tape. We have a computer set-up inside could make Pavarotti sound like Kate Bush.'

Andy climbed up next to his mike, nodding a greeting to Tim and the others. He had a twinge of anxiety as he nodded to Sandra. Her make-up was heavier than ever now, but she still looked ill. All the same, she smiled at him like an angel and her eyes glistened. He found himself wondering about drugs again.

Aaron Priest looked wonderful. He seemed to live in those tight leather trousers and cowboy boots, but had changed his shirt to something sky-blue and frilled. It gave him a dashing, romantic air, as if he was one of the Three Musketeers.

Sammy Walling left the studio and in a moment his voice came over the speakers. 'You hear me all right in there? Aaron, lift your hand.'

Aaron waved lazily towards the glass wall. 'Hear you loud and clear, Sammy,' he said in his soft American accent.

Andy glanced round sharply. How come the producer was talking to Aaron, all of a sudden, and not to the leader of the group?

'OK, take a minute to settle yourselves, then let's have a thirty-second burst so the boys can take levels.'

Andy glanced at the music on his stand and hoisted his guitar. He'd actually started to strum before it suddenly hit him. It wasn't the right music. He'd written a new piece specially for the demo, a soulful, driving ballad called 'Nightwave'

74

designed, although he wished it didn't have to be, as a showcase for Aaron Priest. The *Gravediggers* had rehearsed it thoroughly and it was good. Although it galled Andy to admit it, Priest sounded great. But what was on the stand was something else entirely.

'Sammy,' he called. 'Can you hear me?'

'Yes, I can, Andy. Any problem?'

'My music's wrong. I mean, I've got the wrong music.' There was no title page to his sheets and while the score looked vaguely familiar, it certainly wasn't "Nightwave". 'I sent you round the stuff we're doing a couple of days ago.'

'Change of plan, Andy,' Sammy Walling's voice came back promptly. 'My fault, sorry, told the others before you got here. Meant to tell you, grovelling apologies. What we're doing is "Light My Fire". That's the music you got. OK?'

Andy frowned. 'The old *Doors* number?'

'Sold a million for them in a month,' said Sammy cheerfully.

Andy felt the first faint hint of anger rising, albeit masked by bewilderment. 'That was back in 1959!' he snapped.

'It was 1967 actually,' Sammy told him. 'You got a problem with this, Andy?'

Andy felt his stomach tighten. 'Yes, I think we've got a problem. We planned to do 'Nightwave'. That's what we rehearsed.'

'Yes, I know. Sorry the change is so last-minute.'

'Last-minute isn't the point, Mr Walling,' Andy said stonily. 'The point is we agreed to do "Nightwave". We didn't agree to do some pop tune that's twenty-eight years past its sell-by date!'

'Well, hey,' said Sammy Walling in a tone of sweet reason, 'what do the rest of you think?'

Andy looked round confidently at his fellow *Diggers*. Neither Dave nor Tim would meet his eye. Aaron Priest said, 'I prefer "Light My Fire".'

'See?' Sammy said, 'Aaron prefers it.'

Andy said quietly, 'What's going on here, guys? Dave, Tim – look at me!'

Dave did look at him. 'Maybe he's right, Andy,' he said quietly. 'For a demo you want something the stations know. I mean, something familiar. More chance of a play.'

'Is that what you *really* think?' The anger, bewilderment and frustration were joined by just the hint of a new emotion: rising panic. 'Come on, Dave, you really *believe* that?'

Before Dave could answer, Sammy's voice came over the speakers again. 'I know "Night-wave" is your number, Andy, and you're proud of it. I understand that. You have every right to be. It's a great number. But it just isn't right for your first single.'

'This has got nothing to do with whether it's my number or not my number!' Andy called back angrily. 'I don't care if it's my number – I'm not on some damn ego trip. What I'm saying is we agreed to do one number and now, without a by-your-leave, we're doing another. No consultation, no discussion, nothing!'

'It was discussed with the group, Andy.'

'It wasn't discussed with me!' Andy yelled.

'You weren't here,' said Sammy flatly.

'Hey, chill out, Andy,' Sandra said softly, 'it's only a demo. Your number can lead our album.'

Andy knew his temper was unrolling and once he lost it he'd lose everything. He'd end up screaming abuse and behaving like a prat. 'I got held up, all right? The traffic was bad. You couldn't have waited just a minute to discuss it? I mean, I'm only the leader of the group.'

'All right,' said Sammy, still sweet reason, 'tell you what – we'll take a vote. That suit you? We'll do it like a democracy. Everybody who wants "Light My Fire" stick up a hand.'

Andy looked round in astonishment as the hands went up: Priest and Sandra without hesitation, Dave and Tim more slowly, but up their hands went just the same.

'Now, who wants "Nightwave"?' Sammy asked.

Andy slowly went solo, his mind racing. This might be the *Gravediggers'* big chance. This might be what they'd worked and waited for. But he'd just found out something important, something he hadn't planned for. Now they were heading for the big time, he was losing control of the group he'd founded.

As if reading his mind, Aaron Priest looked over at him and smiled. He had long teeth. To Andy they looked feral, sharp.

EIGHTEEN

The really galling thing was that Sammy Walling turned out to be right. 'Light My Fire' might be a golden oldie, but even Andy had to admit it sounded better than 'Nightwave' that night in the Gemini Studios.

What was even worse was that he had to admit some of the credit – face facts, just about all of the credit – was down to Aaron Priest. The man was unbelievable. He looked and sounded more like Jim Morrison than Jim Morrison ever did and it was Morrison who drove 'Light My Fire' to the top of the charts back in the Sixties.

But it was more than that. Aaron Priest was magic when he was singing. He generated an energy that laid itself down on tape and screamed through the speakers on the playback. You listened and the hairs on your neck crawled.

It was so good Andy must have dreamed about it because he woke up next morning with the sound of Aaron Priest's voice ringing in his ears: *Baby won't you light my fi-uh*! Exactly the way it sounded on 'The Best of the Doors' except better. Almost all the remix albums since Morrison's death used the version of 'Light My Fire' released as the *Doors* second single. But that was a three-minute cut-down. The original Robby Krieger lyric ran to seven minutes with a long instrumental break in the middle. It was this version that Priest sang for the *Gravediggers* launch demo and it sounded fabulous.

Andy's bedsit didn't actually have a bed. He slept surrounded by clutter on a mattress on the floor. That morning he woke slow, listening to Aaron Priest's voice spilling over from his dream, feeling the tiredness in his limbs, the fuzziness in his head, but at the same time knowing there was something he had to do.

He climbed to his feet, rolled the mattress tightly and pushed it into the cupboard with the broken guitar, the even more broken keyboard and several sweaters for when the weather really turned cold. Then he walked up to the bathroom and took a shower. The water was bordering on cold, which meant he'd slept late and the other tenants had run off most of the tank, but at least it woke him up. By the time he got back to his room he knew exactly what he had to do.

Andy thought about it as he dressed. He knew he'd been incredibly lucky that his group had been spotted by Paul Campbell. He knew there were a thousand young musicians who would have given their ears for a contract with Windstorm. He even knew Aaron Priest was a lucky break despite his worries about Sandra – and he had to admit he couldn't *prove* Priest was giving her drugs, whatever his suspicions.

It all added up to a sweet future, but like all sweet things it had its price. Last night when he discovered his group had been pulled out from under him, he realised just how high that price might be.

But only if he let it.

Which was where Andy was standing this morning. He might not be able to sing as well as Aaron Priest or look as good as Aaron Priest. He might not have Paul Campbell's money or Sammy Walling's rock-hard confidence. But he was still the one who brought the *Gravediggers* together, who worked to get them their first gigs, who lay awake nights plotting and scheming about their future. Which made the *Diggers* his group, not Sammy Walling's, not Aaron Priest's, not Windstorm's. Last night he'd been caught unawares and let something happen that should never have happened.

But it wasn't too late to repair the damage.

Andy dressed carefully, a little more formally than usual. He even ran to a shirt and tie. He was outside standing at the bus stop before he remembered he had real money in his pocket since the Windstorm signing. He went back in and, with a feeling of flamboyance, called a cab.

'Where to, guv?' the driver asked as he climbed into the back.

Andy heard himself release an explosive breath as he answered, 'Seventeen Priory Mews – it's over on the south side just off Langston Street.'

He began rehearsing what he planned to say as he paid off the cab, was still rehearsing as he pushed through the glass door.

Then he stopped.

The reception hall was bare. He blinked. There was no longer a desk, let alone the Naomi

Campbell lookalike behind it. There were no pictures on the walls. There was no glass table, no magazines, no beige leather armchairs. Even the carpet was gone. There was nothing now beneath his feet except dusty wooden boards.

The Windstorm offices were empty except for just the barest whiff of cinnamon.

NINETEEN

Andy stood for a long time, not understanding what he was seeing. A fragment of his mind suddenly announced that the designer plaque on the wall outside had been missing as he came in. He'd scarcely noticed, certainly paid no attention. Even now he didn't quite know what it meant.

A grey-haired woman carrying two buckets and a mop emerged from a door behind where the desk had been. She set them down with a sigh. 'You with the new crowd?' she asked. 'Only it's nowhere near ready yet.'

Andy stared at her. She dipped her mop into one bucket then wrung it out. 'Don't understand the work involved, none of them. Never had to do it themselves, do you see? The blokes all has wives to do it for them and them secretaries – well, they're afraid of breaking a nail, aren't they? Bimbos, if you ask me. Bimbos.' She gave him a mischievous grin.

'What happened?' Andy managed at last.

'What happened to who, dear?'

'Windstorm.'

'What's Windstorm?'

'They were the people working here, Windstorm Records.'

The old lady shrugged. 'Oh, I don't know nothing about that. They comes and they goes. I just clean.'

'Where did they go to?'

'Didn't tell me, dear. Amazing, but there it is.' She began to mop down the boards. 'They owe you money or something?'

He supposed they did in a way. At least they would do when the first single went on sale. If it went on sale. Andy felt his mind beginning to whirl. What was going on here?

Something of his confusion must have shown in his face because the cleaning lady said, 'You want to look around, dear? There may be somebody upstairs.'

Andy felt hugely, pathetically, grateful. 'May I? You don't mind?'

'All the same to me, dear. Just so long as you don't steal nuffink.' She gave him that grin again.

'I won't,' Andy promised and went for the lift.

With no Lois to meet him, Andy had nothing to divert him from the grim reality of the second floor. The carpets were gone from here as well. The cut-crystal chandeliers were gone. Incredibly, even the flock wallpaper had been stripped from the walls, which looked chipped and leprous underneath. Why strip the wallpaper? The carpets and the chandeliers you could use, but nobody reused wallpaper.

His footsteps echoed as he walked down the corridor to Paul Campbell's office. The nameplate was gone from the door. Some vestige of good manners, or maybe it was just habit, made him knock. Then without waiting for a reply, he pushed the door.

Campbell's office was empty. Desks gone, Mac gone, control system gone, sound system gone, television set gone. The heavy curtains had disappeared from the windows. The carpet was gone from the floor, the pictures were gone from the walls. The only things left were a simple, old-fashioned black phone on the floor and the little refrigerated drinks cabinet where Campbell had kept the champagne when they signed their contract. Andy went across to the phone and picked it up. To his surprise, it was still connected: a dial tone sounded in his ear like a dying bee.

Andy parked his bottom on the sill and stared through the window. The office overlooked a quiet residential side street planted with a few tired-looking trees. The parked cars were all mid-range sedate family saloons. What was going on? What had happened to Windstorm?

He discovered to his surprise that his hand was shaking. He watched it, wondering what he'd be like at sixty-five if this was the way he reacted to a crisis now. If it really was a crisis. But if it wasn't a crisis, what was it? He'd signed a contract with Windstorm and now Windstorm and everybody connected with it had ... disappeared. Just vanished.

Except they couldn't have just vanished. They had to have gone somewhere. Maybe just moved office ...

Without telling him.

Without telling him? Without telling anybody in their newest group they were moving? Without even mentioning it? Without sending out new address cards, new phone numbers? Come on, Andy, nobody changes offices like that.

But maybe they did. Maybe Windstorm were just inefficient. Maybe there was a slip-up, an oversight. Maybe that's all there was to it.

He clung to the thought because he didn't want to face up to the alternative. He didn't want to discover his whole future, the whole future of the *Gravediggers* had just been flushed down the tubes. Because it could be that, of course. Windstorm had looked impressive, but that didn't mean a thing. Their office space was rented – that was obvious now. The desks and carpets and equipment might all have been leased. Maybe Campbell with his Porsche and Gucci shoes had been a little less than careful with the company coffers. Maybe Windstorm had been over-stretched and now the elastic had snapped.

Andy got up from the windowsill and started to walk slowly back across the empty room. He felt sick and afraid. He couldn't bear to think the *Gravediggers'* one big chance might have come to nothing.

He leaned over to tug open the door of the fridge. It was still plugged in so the light came on, but it was empty except for a scattering of something brown and crumbly in the bottom. Andy frowned.

God alone knew what Campbell had been keeping in his fridge. If Andy hadn't known better, it looked for all the world like soil.

TWENTY

There was no way he could tell them by phone. It simply wasn't fair to destroy all their hopes and dreams like that. All of them had worked hard for this break and now it was gone, the very least he could do was tell them face to face. For his own sake he decided to get them all together. It was more than he could stand to break the same brutal news over and over. He checked his change and found a phone box.

He didn't want to pull the family emergency stunt again so when he called Dave's building site he asked if it was possible to leave a message. The voice that answered this time had a Yorkshire accent and the man said, 'You just tell me what it is, son, and he'll have it in five minutes – I'm going over to see him now anyway.'

'Tell him,' Andy said, 'to come to Andy Clarke's place after work. Bit of a problem and it's urgent.' He felt relieved not to be talking directly to Dave, who would certainly have pushed him to explain.

He cradled the phone then lifted it again and dialled Tim's number. It was engaged. Andy swore, hung up and tried it again. Still engaged. He looked up Sandra's office number but tried

Tim again. This time it rang and Tim answered it at once.

'Tim? Andy. Can you come round to my place after work?'

'Sure,' Tim said easily. 'What's up?'

'I'd rather tell you when I see you,' Andy said. He prayed Tim wouldn't push.

But Tim was full of other news. 'Hey, Andy, I've been looking at a sports car. What do you think?'

A sports car? For a moment Andy was about to ask if Tim was out of his mind, then he remembered Tim still thought the group was headed for the big-time. He was going to be a famous rock star. The sports car went with that, along with a new home for his parents, a new pad for himself, wild parties and a swimming-pool. Andy knew it all – he'd had his own dreams until he walked into the abandoned Windstorm office.

'I think maybe you should wait before signing anything,' he said carefully.

'Not at that stage yet,' Tim told him cheerfully. 'Just looking.'

Andy cradled the phone again. He realised suddenly he still didn't have a number for Aaron Priest and felt faintly guilty when he discovered he didn't care. Maybe Sandra knew how to get in touch with him in time for tonight's meeting. If not, he could always write and let him know afterwards. There was no way he was going back to National Towers, day or night, to find the flat Priest really lived in. He'd had enough of that tower block for the rest of his life.

There were two girls waiting outside the phone box now, but Andy ignored them. He took a deep breath and dialled the number of Sandra's office. 'Sandra Thurston, please,' he said when the receptionist answered.

'I'm sorry, caller,' the girl said briskly. 'Sandra is on sick leave.'

Sick leave? 'She hasn't been in at all today?'

'She hasn't been in for the past week. Is there someone else who can help you?'

'No,' Andy said thoughtfully. 'I'll try her at home.'

Frowning, he dialled Sandra's flat and listened while the phone rang out. He couldn't quite figure what was going on. Sandra hadn't mentioned anything was wrong at the recording session, although she had looked very pale. If she was ill, it explained a lot of things. He was annoyed she hadn't told him though. The last thing he needed was one of the group battling bravely on when she was too ill to go into work.

As he left the phone box one of the girls said loudly, 'She must be very special to keep him on that long!'

Andy ignored her and walked off down the street. He'd skipped breakfast in his enthusiasm to get to Paul Campbell and while his stomach was far too knotted to eat, he desperately wanted a coffee, very hot, very strong, with too much sugar. But he wasn't sure he should take time to get one.

If Sandra wasn't answering her phone, it probably meant she was in bed. He didn't want to disturb her, but at the same time she deserved to be told the bad news as soon as possible. And besides, he wanted to know if she had a number for Priest.

The bus pulled in as Andy was passing the stop and he grabbed it on impulse. Another taxi might have been faster, but he still wasn't used to taxis. And besides, the voice in his mind said sourly as he took his seat, if Paul Campbell's done a runner and Windstorm's out of business, you can't afford taxis any more, can you? One taxi ride. It had been a short sharp taste of the big-time.

He stared out of the window, wondering if their shot at the big-time really was gone. But facts were facts. Paul Campbell had disappeared. The Windstorm offices were deserted, everything stripped out of them. That might just mean a move around the corner, but why hadn't Paul Campbell told anyone? Andy had had too many hard knocks in his life to put a bright interpretation on this situation.

He glanced towards the alleyway as he reached the steps to Sandra's flat. It looked a lot different in daylight and he could now see a fire hydrant that in the dark might just possibly have looked like a cloaked figure. He took the steps two at a time. He had more real worries now than an imaginary cloaked figure.

The name on the bell said simply s. THURSTON with no indication of sex, the usual thing for a girl on her own. Andy thumbed it and waited.

A neat, bearded man in his thirties bounded up the steps, nodded to Andy in a friendly fashion and used his key to open the front door. Andy slipped in gratefully behind him. If she was in bed ill, the chances were she wouldn't answer her bell.

Her door was second on the right. He knocked firmly and waited. The door of the flat across the hall opened and a middle-aged woman with short ash-blonde hair came out carrying a refuse sack. She was wearing an open dressing-gown over a pink nightie and pink slippers. There was a cigarette dangling from the side of her mouth.

'You looking for Sandra, love?' the woman asked. Then, without waiting for a reply, 'You've missed her, I'm afraid. She went out half an hour ago. Want me to give her a message, love? I usually see her if my friend doesn't call to take me out.'

Andy felt a trickle of relief. At least Sandra wasn't too ill to go out. He smiled at the woman. 'No, thank you. I'll put a note under the door.'

'Suit yourself, love,' the woman said and disappeared into her flat.

Andy wrote the message leaning his paper on the wall:

Dear Sandra,
Something's happened. Can you phone me at home about a meeting at my place tonight about 7 after everybody's through with work? If you can't make the meeting I'll tell you what's happened on the phone. Do you have a phone number for Aaron? I need to contact him as well. It's important.
Love,
Andy

He folded it in half and tapped it through the space beneath the door. Then he left the building and caught another bus home.

He heard the communal phone ringing as he walked through the front door. It occurred to him it might be Sandra so he flew up the stairs to answer it. To his astonishment, Paul Campbell's voice crackled down the line. 'That you, Andy? I've been trying to get hold of you all day. I've got news. Are you listening?'

Andy felt his stomach knot even though he already knew Paul Campbell's news. 'I'm listening,' he said.

TWENTY-ONE

The percolator started to pop as Andy did his last-minute tidy-up. It wasn't that he worried about tidiness. It was more that everybody needed somewhere to sit down.

He was feeling an idiot, a condition that was getting all too familiar these days. After the nonsense of the day, after *schlepping* twice across town, calling people and leaving notes, turning life into a crisis, it seemed Windstorm hadn't gone out of business after all.

Not even close, Andy. It was just a move to bigger offices. Why hadn't he been notified? Paul Campbell sounded puzzled – the change of address cards had gone out a week before. Maybe Andy's had got lost in the post. But that didn't matter. Did he have a pen? Here was the new address. And if he lost it, he could always call the old number – calls were transferred automatically.

What a dumbo! How to turn something simple into a nightmare! But at least Paul had bailed him out of making a complete fool of himself. The news *was* breathtaking. Once he heard it, he would have called the meeting anyway.

The doorbell rang as he was stuffing a pair of evil-smelling socks behind a cushion. It had once been possible to open the front door on an electronic buzzer, but the thing had been broken for weeks so Andy raced out and opened the door himself.

Sandra and Aaron Priest were standing on the doorstep. Priest seemed to be wearing the same aftershave as Paul Campbell since there was a whiff of cinnamon about him. Sandra, to his surprise, looked wonderful, still pale, but the rings had gone from round her eyes.

'I thought you were sick,' he said.

'Who told you that?'

'I called you at work. They said you hadn't been in for a week. That's why I left the note.'

'Come on, Andy,' Sandra asked, smiling, 'You think I'm sticking in that dead-end job now we've got a recording contract? They'll be lucky if they ever see me again. Aren't you going to invite us in?'

'Oh, yes, sure thing. Come in! Come in!'

'We shared a taxi,' Sandra said inconsequentially. The Windstorm contract again.

'Hi, Andy,' Priest said. He stopped suddenly and looked around as he stepped into the bedsit. Eventually he said, 'Interesting pad.'

Andy shrugged. Priest made him feel inferior, but he was determined not to show it. 'I'm looking round for somewhere better.'

'No, really, I like it. I like lots of things around me.'

Could have fooled me, Andy thought remembering Priest's flat, then remembering it wasn't Priest's flat at all, but the wrong address altogether. He wondered who it really belonged

93

to. He wondered if Sandra knew. He wondered how she'd given him the wrong address.

He hated the fact she'd arrived with Priest.

'Are we the first here?' Sandra asked, although it was perfectly obvious they were. 'What's it all about, Andy? Your note sounded really mysterious.' She flashed him a smile that sent his hormones racing. 'Something good I hope.'

Andy smiled back and jiggled his hand cautiously in the air. 'Well, maybe not bad,' he said. 'But I'd better wait until the others arrive.'

'I think that may be them now,' said Priest as the doorbell rang again.

Andy glanced at him. He could have sworn Priest had started speaking *before* the bell sounded. Except he couldn't have unless he was psychic. Andy went off to open the front door. It was Dave.

'There's trouble, isn't there?' Dave asked at once. 'I could tell by your message. What's happened? It's bad, isn't it? Here, don't close that – Tim's just coming.'

Andy pulled the front door open again. Tim was climbing the steps. To Dave, Andy said, 'It's not trouble, Dave. Far from it. Go on in – Sandra and Aaron are inside.'

'Not bad news? You sure?' But he went through as Andy greeted Tim.

'Anybody want coffee?' Andy asked when they were all together.

'I'm looking after that,' Sandra said. She had cups lined up and was already filling them from the percolator. 'Why don't you just get on with telling us what this is all about?'

'All right,' Andy said. He licked his lips. After the morning's panic, he was determined to come across cool and professional so he said, 'Couple of things. First, I want to congratulate you all on the recording. As you know, I wasn't happy with the choice of "Light My Fire" and I'm still not happy about the way it happened. But I have to tell you I was wrong about the number. It didn't just work, it worked better than "Nightwave" Congratulations.' He hesitated, then added, 'Especially to you, Aaron. The way you hit that piece was the best I've ever heard.' Well, there, he'd finally done it. He'd said something nice to Aaron Priest in public.

'Yeah, yeah, yeah,' Sandra grinned, 'and you called us all together here just to tell us how great we were?'

'No,' Andy said, 'I called you all together to help me drink these.' He reached behind the curtain and produced two bottles of champagne. 'They're not as good as the stuff Campbell gave us and they're a bit warm, I'm afraid, because I don't have a fridge, and you'll have to have paper cups because I don't have champagne glasses, but apart from that we have another celebration!'

Dave looked at him. 'Two bottles? Just because you were wrong about "Nightwave"?'

'Earlier today I got a call from Paul Campbell,' Andy told them. 'Windstorm's just moved office, incidentally, so he was calling from their new place. Anyway, despite having their hands full, Windstorm has been making some very interesting plans.'

'Well, come on,' Dave urged. 'Let's hear the worst!'

'That was a dramatic pause,' Andy told him. 'That was to bring a little excitement to our otherwise drab lives.'

'Get to the bottom line,' Dave growled.

'The bottom line is that Windstorm are going to follow up our demo single with an album,' Andy said. 'The big news is they want it to be recorded at our live concert.'

'We're not booked for any live concert,' Dave said.

Andy waited for the penny to drop.

TWENTY-TWO

At first they couldn't believe it.

'Windstorm's organising a live concert for us?' Dave asked with the sort of look on his face that said he was delighted but afraid he must have misheard.

'That's right,' Andy said.

'Where?'

'Venue to be confirmed,' Andy said.

'Doesn't matter,' Tim said. He was grinning and hugging himself. 'God this is fast! Isn't this fast, Andy?'

'It's fast all right,' Andy agreed. He started to struggle with a champagne cork. 'Windstorm will be looking after all the expenses, all the publicity. All we have to do is come on and play.' He was stringing it out, holding back the best to the last.

'Hey,' Dave said, 'that's cool!'

'And there'll be a lot of publicity,' Andy said.

It was Sandra who picked up on it. She cocked her head to one side. 'You're not telling us everything, Andy.'

'Aren't I?' Andy asked innocently. 'What could I have left out?'

'Come on, Andy!' Sandra said. 'What is it?'

Andy decided he couldn't string it out any

longer. 'I think maybe you'd better sit down for this.'

They stared at him expectantly. 'We are sitting,' Dave pointed out.

'Paul had an idea. The demo single is our launch, but even if it goes well, it's no guarantee the album will go well too—'

'It'll depend what's in it,' Dave interrupted with a frown. 'I mean, if you have the numbers, it will sell. That's always been the way.'

'Nobody's arguing, Dave,' Andy told him. 'But Paul has this idea that we cut an album of a live concert and don't get me wrong, it's *our* concert, the *Gravediggers* get star billing, but we're joined by a couple of top-name stars.'

'Like, rock stars?' Dave asked.

'Playing with us, singing with us, joshing around with us, introducing us, telling everybody how great we are – the whole works!' Andy said. He could hardly believe it himself, but Campbell had insisted it was a done deal. Or would be.

They stared at him. Even Dave was stunned into silence.

Eventually Sandra asked, 'Who?'

'Our guest stars?' Andy shrugged. 'Paul wouldn't give me names. He wants to wait until they're signed up. But he's – ' He actually hesitated. It still seemed too good to be true. Then he went on, 'I think he's after somebody from the *Stones*.'

'*The Stones?*' Tim echoed.

'This is the *Rolling* Stones?' Dave asked incredulously. 'I mean, we're not talking about Joe Stones and his Hillbilly Wingwangs, are we?'

'We're talking about the *Rolling Stones*,' Andy said. 'As in Mick Jagger, Bill Wyman, Keith Richards, Charlie Watts, Ron Wood type *Rolling Stones*. At least that's what Campbell says.'

'Somebody from the *Rolling Stones*,' Dave echoed. He looked as though he'd just been hit on the head with a baseball bat.

Sandra said, 'This could make us.'

'Oh, yes,' Andy said soberly, 'I know.'

He managed to pop the champagne cork at last and hurriedly poured it into the paper cups before it foamed on to the floor.

Twenty-Three

The down side was Sandra left with Aaron.

Andy had some stupid fantasy that now things were going so right, now they were cutting an album and playing live with somebody from the *Rolling Stones*, now he'd shown he could negotiate the opportunities of a lifetime, she might throw herself into his arms and tell him she'd had enough of taking it slowly so why couldn't they become an item?

He thought of their first kiss, which had turned out to be their last. She'd wanted to take it slowly then and she hadn't gone out with him since. He'd never fooled himself about the reason, but that didn't mean he liked it. Somehow he thought he'd feel a lot better if she'd fallen for Dave or Tim. Anybody but Priest. The stupid thing was, he didn't know why he disliked Priest so much. Unless it was simply that Sandra had fallen for him.

The others left and Andy dropped the empty champagne bottles in the bin. He'd drunk very little and his head was clear. This was the part of the evening he dreaded. It was crazy. He was facing the biggest opportunity of his entire life, a chance for more money and fame than he'd ever dared dream about, and now, with the gang gone, he was feeling lonely and miserable.

All because Sandra left with Aaron Priest.

Who smells of cinnamon, the voice said in his head.

Andy sighed. It had been a while since the voice popped up, but he was interested to note it still came up with the stupidest of stupid remarks. So Aaron Priest smelled of cinnamon, so what? Everybody seemed to smell of cinnamon these days. Paul Campbell, Windstorm offices ... he'd even thought he caught a whiff of it from Sandra earlier, although that was probably because she'd been snogging Priest and picked up a little of his aftershave.

Even when you started with cinnamon, you still came back to Sandra's relationship with Aaron Priest. On impulse, Andy grabbed his coat and raced out of the flat. He needed to find somewhere with people.

The coffee bar was less than half full. He ordered a cappuccino and helped himself to a chocolate muffin, then found an empty table in a corner and sat down facing the door. He half hoped he might see somebody he knew, but none of the faces were familiar.

He started to feel seriously sorry for himself. For as long as he could remember he'd wanted to be a rock star. At school when his friends were hassling about teacher training courses and degrees in engineering, he was sneaking off to practise guitar. When they were chasing after girls, he was – well, he was chasing after girls too, but he was also chasing after anybody who looked like they had musical talent.

There had been a couple of false starts. The Hughes Twins, Nick and Albert, had talent. Nick played guitar, Albert played absolutely anything he got his hands on and was brilliant on a keyboard. But neither of them had a scrap of dedication. They turned up for rehearsal or didn't as the fancy took them. Colin Kent had been a disaster as well. Nice singing voice, but at seventeen he already had a drug habit. You could never tell whether he was going to stand up at the microphone or fall down.

He'd found Dave Anderton eventually, Mr Pessimism himself, but with the necessary combination of talent, ambition and reliability. After Dave appeared, Tim turned up as if by magic and suddenly Andy had a mini group. They discussed names endlessly and went through three incarnations before settling on the *Gravediggers*. Once Andy got his booking at the Crescent Club everything had started to move like a juggernaut rolling downhill.

Now the *Gravediggers* had already cut their first single, were going to make their first album, and were heading for their first major concert, introduced, if you could believe it, by Mick Jagger or Keith Richards or somebody of that ilk. He ought to have been swinging from the chandelier, but instead he was sitting alone in a coffee bar, dosing up on sugar and feeling like something that had just dropped out of the wrong end of a Rottweiler.

He finished his coffee, stuffed the last of the

muffin into his mouth and got up to go. He had to get his head together, otherwise the rest of the evening was going to be a total misery. Maybe a walk would help.

Outside it had begun to rain, not hard, but a soaking drizzle that had cleared the street completely. Andy turned up his collar and put his head down grimly. Even the weather had turned foul to suit his mood. He had walked less than a hundred metres when he heard the commotion in the sidestreet.

Andy glanced down. The sidestreet was badly lit, but there was more than enough light to see what was going on. Two youths had someone on the ground and were kicking him viciously.

'Hey!' Andy called. 'Hey, what do you think you're doing?' He started to run down the sidestreet. The youths took a quick glance in his direction, gave the prostrate form a final kick, then ran off.

Andy dropped to one knee beside the body on the ground. 'Are you all right?' he asked stupidly. It was a man about his own age, his face bruised and bloody. A cut on his scalp was bleeding profusely. Andy dug a handkerchief out of his pocket and cradled the man's head. 'Hold still,' he told him firmly. 'I want to make sure you've no bones broken. And get you cleaned up a bit.'

As Andy wiped away the blood, he realised suddenly that he knew this man. He was the skinhead with the swastika tattooed on his scalp. The one who'd sent him to the wrong flat when he was looking for Aaron Priest.

TWENTY-FOUR

Andy was still half carrying the man as he opened the door to his bedsit. He wasn't sure he should be bringing him back at all, but couldn't really see any alternative. The skinhead was still bleeding through the packed handkerchief held to his wound. He needed a doctor and the nearest phone was at Andy's place.

Andy gently set him in a chair, propping him so he didn't slump. 'Take it easy,' he said quietly. 'I'm just going up to phone a doctor.'

'No doctor, Jimmy,' the skinhead mumbled.

Andy stopped. 'Come on, you need that cut seen to. And the police should be notified – those two shouldn't get away with this.'

Despite his wound, the skinhead actually grinned. 'Definitely no police.' He shifted painfully in the chair. 'Just let me sit here a minute and I'll be all right.'

Andy went over to the sink and squeezed out a cloth in warm water. He brought it back and started to clean the blood off the man's face. The scalp wound was the worst, although his nose was bleeding too, but both seemed to be clotting now at long last. 'Any chest pain?' The kicking had been vicious and he was wondering about broken ribs.

The skinhead grinned again. 'What do you think, Sunshine?'

'I think you should have a doctor look you over.'

'Ah, it's only bruising. No need to waste the time of the medical profession. Or the legal profession. Especially the legal profession. You let me sit here for five minutes and I'll be on my way, leave you alone, get back to your life.' He pushed himself more upright in the chair and looked at Andy's face for the first time. 'Here, I know you. You were the fella looking for the Yank.'

Andy nodded. 'And you were the fellow sent me to the wrong place.'

The skinhead looked at him for a long time then said, 'The name's Vernon Harrison, but anybody calls me Vernon gets a bunch of fives.'

'What do they call you if they don't want a bunch of fives?' Andy asked.

'Snuff,' Vernon told him.

Andy said cautiously, 'Andy Clarke.' Formal introductions seemed a bit odd under the circumstances.

'What's this about the wrong place, Andy?' Snuff asked quietly.

'You sent me to the wrong flat,' Andy said. 'I was looking for Aaron Priest.'

'The Yank? Looks like Jim Morrison?'

Andy nodded. 'Yes.'

'I sent you to the right place all right,' Snuff said. 'You just got lucky he wasn't in.'

'What's that supposed to mean?'

'It's supposed to mean Priest's bad news,'

Snuff said. He started to push himself painfully to his feet. Andy reached out to help, but he waved him away. After a moment he was standing, swaying slightly. 'See?' he said. 'Right as rain!'

'Are you sure you don't want me to call a doctor?'

Snuff smiled thinly. 'Doctors ask too many questions, know what I mean?' He was running his hands cautiously over his sides. 'Don't think there's any serious damage.' He looked at Andy. 'Word of advice?'

'What?'

'Don't get mixed up with that fella. You see him coming, cross the street.'

'I'm already mixed up with him,' Andy said. 'We're both in the same rock group.'

Snuff released his breath explosively. ' Jesus!' he said. 'The bastard's in a rock group. Just like Lestat. Can you get rid of him?'

Andy blinked. 'Get rid of him?'

'Throw him out. Can you give him his marching papers, Jimmy? Tell him if he comes back you'll kick the living—'

'He's our lead singer,' Andy said.

Snuff looked away from him and sighed. 'Nobody ever believes it.' He turned back. 'Sunshine, you're in more trouble than you know.'

What Andy was feeling was fear. He was feeling confusion as well, bewilderment even, but most of what he was feeling was fear. Everything this man said was making him feel more nervous. Because he was feeling nervous, he said defensively, 'We're actually doing well – the group. We've been doing well since Aaron joined.'

Snuff cut him off. 'Listen, Andy, I like you. You stopped those two clowns before they did me serious damage, know what I mean? So I owe you. If you're getting yourself mixed up with the Yank, you're going to need this.' He pulled something from his pocket and placed it on the table.

Andy picked it up. It was a cheap religious medallion with a brassy glint that was probably supposed to look like gold. One side showed a plump little saint with a halo, his eyes raised, his hands clasped in prayer. Andy turned it over. On the back were the words: A BLESSING FOR YOUR GOODNESS.

'Take it,' Snuff said soberly. 'It might help you see things the way they really are.

Andy looked at the medallion. Help what? Help how? Snuff was making no sense at all. 'I'm not a Catholic,' he said eventually. He assumed the thing was Catholic – it looked like the sort of souvenir people brought back from Lourdes. 'I don't believe in this sort of stuff.'

'Neither do I,' Snuff said without a flicker of expression. 'But the Catholics tell me it works whether you believe in it or not.' He moved over to the door. 'Thanks for the help, Sunshine. Much appreciated. Think about getting rid of Priest.'

Andy sat staring at the clutter of his bedsit long after Snuff was gone. He was still bewildered by the conversation, but the whole tone had left him far more nervous than he'd felt in months. The big puzzle was the medallion. Why would a skinhead who didn't believe in these things give him a religious medallion? Why give him a medallion even if he had believed in it? Snuff obviously thought Priest was trouble, but what sort of trouble was sorted out with a religious medallion?

While he was still chewing on the mystery of the medallion, Andy suddenly discovered he'd solved another part of the puzzle altogether. Sandra said she'd given him the wrong address. Snuff insisted he'd sent Andy to the right flat. At first it seemed like one of them must be lying or mistaken, but now Andy suddenly realised both could be telling the truth.

When he went to National Towers, he'd counted the doors to find the flat number Sandra gave him. He was actually knocking on the door as Snuff and his mates arrived. When Snuff sent him to another door, Andy had assumed he'd made a mistake. But suppose he hadn't? Suppose he'd worked out the number correctly and was knocking at the number Sandra gave him? That meant, according to both Snuff and Sandra, he was at the wrong door. Snuff had sent him to the right one. Simple.

He suddenly found he was feeling relieved. He hadn't realised he'd been doubting Sandra, but he must have been. And now it was nice to know those doubts were groundless. Then the relief drained away. Because if Snuff *had* sent him to the right door, then Aaron Priest really did live with a coffin in his flat and that freaky tray of soil in his fridge.

Hard on the heels of this thought came another

in the form of a recent memory. The voice in his head quietly replayed a fragment of Snuff's conversation:

'The bastard's in a rock group. Just like Lestat.'

Just like Lestat. Just like Lestat. It had slid right past Andy when Snuff said it, but now Andy remembered who Lestat was. The dark, pop-singing hero of Anne Rice's *Vampire Chronicles*.

Which meant Snuff thought Priest was a vampire too.

TWENTY-FIVE

It all looked different in the morning. It was one thing to believe – well, half believe – in vampires in the middle of the night. It was quite another when you woke up to the cold light of day with glued eyes, a furred mouth and five coffee cups needing washing. Andy crawled to the bathroom, showered thoroughly and thought about it.

First off, there were no such things as vampires. It didn't matter if you lived with a coffin and kept a tray of earth in your fridge – none of that made you a vampire. Even sleeping in a coffin didn't make you a blood-drinker. Tim's great-aunt had slept in a coffin and the only thing she drank was tea.

As Andy stepped out of the shower, he realised he'd convinced himself. Nothing he'd seen in Priest's flat made him anything more than a poor housekeeper.

He was just stepping into his boxers when the doorbell rang.

To his astonishment, Paul Campbell was standing on the doorstep. Two wheels of his Porsche were pulled up on the pavement.

'Hi, Andy,' Paul said. 'Glad I caught you.' He

pushed past into the hallway, looked around vaguely.

Andy closed the front door and pointed to the open door of his bedsit. 'In here, Paul.'

Paul stepped through. 'Wow, Andy, I'm not paying you enough. This place is a *tip*!'

'I'm looking round,' Andy said apologetically. He discovered a chair that didn't have grot on it and gestured Paul to sit down. 'Can I make you coffee?'

'Is it instant?'

'Afraid so,' Andy said. He'd run out of ground coffee the night before.

'I think I'll pass,' Paul told him. He kept looking round the room. 'You know, Andy, you really can get away from this place now. It's not just that you deserve better, it's a question of image. Living one step up from a squat doesn't suit your image, doesn't suit Windstorm's image. Tell you what—' He stopped.

'What?' Andy asked.

'The company owns a block of flats on the south side. As far as I remember, two of them are vacant at the moment and one's becoming vacant next month. They've all much the same accommodation – two bedrooms, living-room, modern kitchen with breakfast bar, big bathroom with bath, loo and shower, phone, gas central heating, usual thing. But to give them an edge, we don't just furnish them, we put in a TV and sound system – wholesale to us so it doesn't cost much – and a selection of Windstorm discs and cassettes for, you know, PR. We're very selective about our tenants – that's why there are vacancies. But you could have your pick, move in next week if you like.'

Andy stared at him. Finally he said, 'Hey, I don't think I could afford a pad like that on the south side, even with the money I'll be earning from Windstorm.'

'Sure you can,' Paul said. He grinned. 'They're subsidised for Windstorm artists. How much are you paying here?'

Andy told him. Paul shrugged. 'Fiver a week more – you can afford that, can't you?'

Stunned, Andy said, 'I could afford more. I mean – Are you serious? Another twenty a month and I can have a place on the south side with two bedrooms, its own bath and a free stereo system?'

'I'm serious all right. How do you think I'd feel when the columnist from *Rolling Stone* comes round to interview Windstorm's latest acquisition and finds you living in this tip? You want people to take you seriously, Andy, you have to look the part. I'll be putting the same deal to the others, of course, but – ' he glanced around again in obvious distaste, ' – your situation looks the most urgent. You want me to organise a viewing? I don't actually look after our property division myself.'

Andy pushed a heap of magazines to one side and sat down. 'Thanks. Thanks, Paul. Wow. Yes. Yes, organise it. Heck, tell whoever I'll take one. Any of them.'

'Look at them first,' Paul Campbell advised. 'You might as well have the view you like. And, incidentally, you don't like the decor or the colour of the carpet, we'll change it. Nothing but the best for Windstorm's boys.'

'I don't know what to say,' Andy said.

'Then don't say anything,' said Paul. 'This isn't generosity – if we keep our people happy, they work better, don't go running off to some other label. Everybody makes money.' He shifted in his chair. 'Anyway, I didn't come here to talk about property.'

'I'm sorry,' Andy said, 'I'm not even dressed.'

'It's not illegal. Listen, did you tell the others about the concert?'

'Last night.'

'How did they take it?'

Andy smiled at him. 'They were over the moon. How else would they take it?'

Paul sniffed. 'Never can tell when you're dealing with creative people. They might have thought they'd be overshadowed by the couple of big names. Some kids are funny like that.'

'No problem with us,' Andy assured him. 'Can you tell me who you're getting?'

'Not yet,' Paul said. 'In fact I'm not sure I won't keep that under my hat when I do know. That way you won't get nervous. Meet them on the night.'

'I'd get nervous meeting them on the night.'

'No you won't. Most of the really big stars are nice people. Anyway, I can tell you something – venue and the date. You'll be playing at Kersten Stadium.'

Andy blinked. 'Where?'

'Never heard of it? I'm not surprised. It's out of town. The thing is, we need somewhere big

113

enough to hold the crowds. This gig is going to be huge. Kersten was originally built as a sports complex. That's why it's got the size. We want the concert on the 28th.'

For a minute Andy thought he had misheard, then realised he had misunderstood. 'The 28th of next month,' he said.

But Paul shook his head. 'Of this month.'

Andy felt his mouth drop open and discovered he could do nothing about it. Eventually, in rising panic, he said, 'But that's two *weeks*!'

'Do you have a problem with that?' Paul asked him calmly.

'Of course I have a problem with that!' Andy exclaimed. 'We have to work out a programme. We have to rehearse.' A thought struck him and he added, 'You won't be able to advertise it and distribute tickets in time.'

'You leave that to us,' Paul said easily. 'I'm here to find out if you can do your bit.'

'Get a programme together? Rehearse?'

'Yes.'

'Well, we can put a programme together so long as you don't want new material – '

'We don't.'

'It'll be tight,' Andy said.

'I don't doubt that,' Paul said, 'but can you do it? Andy, I heard you weren't happy about a decision being taken behind your back when we were cutting the single. That's why I'm here now. So we can work any problems out between us, you and I. Can you do it?'

After a long pause Andy said reluctantly, 'Just about.' His head was racing already, trying to get some shape on the million things he had to do.

Paul Campbell smiled. For some reason at that moment his expression reminded Andy of Aaron Priest. If he'd had time to think about it, he might have suspected it was the teeth.

TWENTY-SIX

Life turned into a whirl for Andy. Looking back, it was a series of blurred images surrounded by confusion.

There was the courier, a youth in motorcycle gear who held his finger firmly on Andy's bell until Andy opened the door then asked through his adenoids, 'You Andy Clarke? Sign here.'

Andy took the clipboard and signed the top copy without even reading it. The courier handed him an envelope, saluted and left. Andy opened the envelope on the way back into his bedsit. It contained several sheets of paper and a business card. The card was Paul Campbell's, identifying him as Chief Executive of Windstorm Records. The papers were a photostat of a contract with somebody called Masters Property Development for the hire of Kersten Stadium on the 28th.

Paul didn't want them rehearsing at *Make Mine Music* any more. Windstorm had just taken over its own set of luxury rehearsal rooms and he wanted the *Gravediggers* to use them instead. Now Andy was standing outside them supervising while workmen moved in the last of the gear.

It was new. It was top of the range. It must have cost a fortune.

'Careful,' Andy called, maybe for the hundred-thousandth time. He was nervous as a kitten. In his most optimistic moments he hadn't dreamed of using gear like this. Now he saw it being carted through the double doors and still did not believe it.

Eventually the stream of equipment dried up. A grey-haired foreman in a brown overall coat approached him. 'Sign here, son.'

'What's this?' Andy asked.

'Delivery docket,' the man said.

Andy signed with just the barest hesitation. He was only signing for delivery. He wasn't admitting responsibility for gear that had to be valued at tens, maybe even hundreds, of thousands of pounds.

'Welcome to my humble Abud!' said Andy expansively, even though they were a million miles away from *Make Mine Music* now. Old habits died hard and besides, he was superstitious. First one at rehearsal, always said '*Welcome to my humble Abud.*' It would be bad luck not to.

'Wow,' Tim said, 'look at that equipment!'

'I don't think we're going to make it on time,' Dave said. 'We've only just over a week to get the programme together – it's impossible, Andy, just plain impossible.'

'We're going to have to try, Dave,' Andy told him.

'Yeah,' Dave said gloomily, 'but it isn't going to work.'

'Yes it is,' Andy said firmly. 'We're just going to have to make it work.'

This time it was late at night, well after rehearsals finished for the day and Andy, exhausted, was hunched over a card-table with felt-tip and a big, old, feint-lined yellow pad, trying to put some shape to the show.

Nobody had told him what size of an audience was expected, but it had to be big. Far beyond anything the *Gravediggers* had played to before. Far beyond anything in Andy's personal experience. He suspected he'd never even been to a concert with an audience that would match the one they would face in a few days time. What sort of programme would go down with an audience like that? What sort of numbers would they expect to hear?

The group had been rehearsing rock classics, starting with 'Light My Fire' because Aaron was so good at that one. They sounded great – Andy had no worries on that score. And he had no worries about the numbers. Everybody agreed it should be classics. Paul Campbell wanted classics, Sammy Walling (who, Andy assumed, would be producing the technical recording of the concert) wanted classics, all God's children wanted classics, so who was Andy Clarke to argue?

But what order should the programme run? What number should come first? What number should come last? How did you get the balance right? Did you follow a lively number with something softer? Did you work in sets like a dance? When did you take a break?

He wrote out programme after programme, varying the order, trying one thing then another. He tore pages from the pad, crumpled them and threw them into the chaos of his bedsit. His head grew heavier and heavier until finally he slumped over the card table and sank into a dreamless sleep.

He woke feeling a whole lot better. It occurred to him that the size of the audience didn't matter. What mattered was the sort of people who'd be there. And the sort of people who were coming to the concert would be rock fans, the same sort of people who had come to hear the *Gravediggers* right from the beginning. Which meant Andy could stop worrying and start drawing up a programme he knew would work.

It was only five o'clock in the morning, but he started on it right away.

The rehearsal was well underway, the volume was high, everybody was sweating. Aaron Priest stepped up to the mike looking more like Jim Morrison than ever, oozing raw sex appeal, his eyes hooded like a lizard. He pulled the mike off its stand, cradled it between both hands and murmured, 'Pretty good, pretty good!' He looked very, very pleased.

Weary, bleary, with a head full of rock music that just wouldn't switch itself off, eyes blinking in the bright sunshine, Andy walked into the courtyard of a fine old building in a residential district distinguished by the number of Mercs and Ferraris parked along the roadside. In the courtyard itself were parked a vintage Bentley and a brand new Rolls.

He was looking round for the entrance when a young man with lank blond hair materialised at his elbow. He was wearing a midnight blue sharkskin suit he somehow contrived to make look casual. 'Andy Clarke?'

'Yes ?'

'Had to be.' The young man stuck out his hand. 'Bill Mercier, Windstorm Properties. Paul told me you'd be dropping by.' He led Andy into the building, talking as they walked. 'Windstorm springs for a cleaning lady to come in twice a week and muck you out, so you don't have to worry about that sort of crap. But if you're on your own, you'll want something manageable – right?'

'Yea, right,' Andy agreed, feeling mildly poleaxed.

He was shown three apartments, all of them about twenty billion times better than where he was living now.

'I can have any of these?' he asked cautiously.

'Sure. You get first pick. Paul's going to offer what's left to your friends in the group.'

He swallowed 'All at the subsidised rent?'

'Definitely.'

Andy picked the one with the best view.

TWENTY-SEVEN

Kersten Stadium was immense: the seats stretched all the way to a distant horizon and every one was full. But instead of the youngsters Andy would have expected, they were filled with middle aged and elderly people. Nobody was under fifty and several of the older ones looked ill. Their faces had a greenish tinge.

Andy felt his stomach tighten. For some reason he could not remember a thing about how he got here, could not remember the lead-up to the concert, the final rehearsal, nothing. It was as if something had lifted him bodily out of his life and set him down, complete with guitar, on the floodlit stage.

Aaron Priest stepped on to the stage to a patter of polite applause. He was wearing a long black cloak over his familiar leather pants and frilled white shirt. Andy stared at the cloak. He had the strangest feeling he'd seen it before. Then he remembered. This was the cloak worn by the thing that had been standing in the alleyway watching Sandra's flat.

Priest grinned out over the ancient audience which at once fell deathly silent. Andy played a riff on his guitar to try to warm them up a little. It didn't work.

'I am the Lizard King,' Priest announced. 'I can do anything!'

Andy played another riff. There was still no sound from the vast, green-faced audience. Priest was really playing up the Jim Morrison likeness, Andy thought. Morrison used to call himself the Lizard King.

Aaron Priest walked across the stage to Sandra, his cowboy boots echoing in the silence. His grin changed into a fully-fledged smile. Andy noticed how long and sharp his teeth were.

Snuff tugged at Andy's sleeve. 'See what I mean?' he said, nodding his tattooed head in Priest's direction. 'You want to watch out for that fella.'

Priest's tongue flicked out and it was long and forked, like the tongue of a lizard. Reptile scales seemed to have grown on the backs of his hands, on his forehead and cheeks.

'I am the Lizard King,' Priest said again. His eyes were shining. He was standing close to Sandra.

Suddenly Andy began to feel very much afraid. He turned and handed his guitar to Snuff, then hurled himself across the stage. But for some reason all his movements were in slow motion. Out of the corner of his eye he saw Paul Campbell seated in the front row. He had exchanged his trendy gear and Gucci shoes for a fantasy outfit in black vinyl that made him look unbearably evil.

Aaron Priest reached for Sandra, drew her to

him like a lover. His mouth, with its long, sharp teeth, opened very wide.

'Nooooo!' screamed Andy as Aaron bent to puncture the delicate blue vein throbbing at her throat. From the front row, Paul Campbell started to applaud. In seconds the entire audience had followed his example, clapping, screaming, stamping their feet wildly.

Andy woke up, heart pounding fiercely, his body slick with sweat. Through the bedroom window of his new pad he could see the sun just rising.

It was the day of the *Gravediggers* celebrity concert at Kersten Stadium.

TWENTY-EIGHT

Andy walked naked from the bedroom of his new apartment into the *en suite* bathroom. The central heating had come on automatically. There was carpet beneath his feet. Best of all, he wouldn't meet another tenant in the corridor, because he wasn't in the corridor. He could visit the bathroom without ever leaving his flat.

The shower was hot. Not warm like the shower up the stairs from his old bedsit, nor cold because he'd overslept and the other tenants had drained the tank. This was an electric shower that heated its own water – and pumped it too, to judge from the pressure.

He dried himself with an enormous towel – bed linen and towels had been provided by Windstorm – warm from a heated rail. He stared at his reflection for a moment in the tinted mirror (which somehow contrived to make him look good) then walked to the bedroom to dress.

There were new clothes in the wardrobe. They didn't exactly come with the flat, but they'd been chosen by Paul Campbell and paid for by Windstorm. The message on Andy's answerphone – Andy had an answerphone now – explained it was a question of image and Paul hoped Andy didn't mind.

Andy didn't. It was gear he'd have died for and when he tried it on, it fitted perfectly. He wondered how Paul had got his measurements.

He rustled up a light breakfast using an electric hob that had more controls than the launch console at Cape Canaveral. He dropped bread into the toaster and watched it pop the second it was brown. He started up a brand-new coffee-maker that made his old percolator look like a toy.

As he sat down to eat, he pressed a button on a remote control that not only switched on one of the flat's two television sets, but actually brought it sliding out from behind a concealed panel with a faint hydraulic hiss. The same remote controlled a sound system wired discreetly through to every room, but Andy fancied watching breakfast TV this morning because Paula Yates was on.

He thought she might stop him worrying about the concert.

After breakfast he shaved, then brought in the post. With it came a morning paper and the latest copy of *Rolling Stone*. There seemed to be a newspaper delivery to each of the flats, but it looked as if somebody had taken out a subscription to the magazine in his name. No prizes for guessing who that somebody might be.

Andy put his cowboy boots – Paul Campbell had bought him several pairs of cowboy boots a bit like Aaron's – up on the glass-topped coffee table and settled back in the leather armchair to read. There was a huge ad for the *Gravediggers'* concert on page five. It promised guest appearances by two unnamed top rock stars.

Mid-morning the phone rang. 'Hi, Andy,' said Paul Campbell's voice. 'Coping?'

'Just about,' Andy said.

'You're going to be terrific, absolutely great. I have faith in you, my man.'

'Thanks, Paul. Wish I had.'

'Everybody gets nerves before a big performance,' Paul said. 'I was just talking to Mick and he tells me the same thing after all these years. Nerves beforehand, but they disappear as soon as you come on stage.'

'Mick? Mick Jagger? Is he coming?'

'Did I say that?' Paul asked. 'I told you I wasn't going to let you know until you got there. But it might be Mick. It's definitely one of the *Rolling Stones* ... Might have somebody from *Queen* ...'

'Paul, this is really incredible. I don't know how to thank you enough.'

And then Paul said something very strange. He said, 'So you'll definitely be coming, Andy? You'll definitely be there?'

For half a beat Andy wondered if he'd misheard, but the line was clear as a bell. 'What are you talking about, Paul?' he asked. 'Of course I'll be there!'

'I think I'd like to hear you say it, Andy. I think I'd like to hear you say, "I'll definitely be at the Kersten Stadium tonight and I'll be coming of my own free will." There was an odd quality

126

to Paul's voice, anxiety overlaid with ... well, with hunger.

'Paul, what is this?' Andy frowned.

Harshly, Paul snapped, 'Just say it!'

'I'll definitely be at the Kersten Stadium tonight, Paul. Of course I will. Where else would I be?'

"And I'll be coming of my own free will." Say it!'

'Paul—'

'Say it, damn you! Say it!'

'All right, all right! I'll be coming of my own free will! Just try to keep me away, man! Paul, what's wrong?'

There was silence for a moment that stretched all the way to eternity and back. When Paul spoke again he actually sounded relieved. 'Hey, don't mind me. I'm just wired. I've invested a lot in this gig. I mean, Windstorm has spent ... you don't want to hear. I just want to make sure everything goes smoothly. I'll have the limo pick you up at six. It'll take an hour to get to the stadium.'

'Limo?' Andy echoed.

'Sure. How else should a rock star travel?'

'You're sending a limo to pick up the group?'

'I'm sending limos to pick up each member of the group,' Paul corrected him. 'You keep forgetting I believe in image.'

'Paul, I—' He stopped, completely at a loss.

'Listen, Andy,' Paul said. 'Tonight you get the treatment. Stretch limo, darkened windows, uniformed chauffeur, bar and satellite TV in the back, you name it.'

'Paul, I . . . don't know what to say.'

'Then say nothing,' Paul advised. 'Just be ready on time.'

'I promise,' Andy said.

The phone rang again just as he put it down. He picked it up and found himself talking to Sandra. Her voice sounded distant, muffled and distorted as if she was speaking from the bottom of a galvanised tank. 'Andy, I was just checking you were coming tonight.'

Andy took the phone from his ear and stared at it for a moment. Another one wondering if he was coming tonight. What was the matter with everybody? If he was struck down by a comet he'd have the pieces of his body shipped to Kersten Stadium tonight.

'I'll be there. How about you?'

She missed the sarcasm and said seriously, 'Try to stop me. Paul's sending limos – did you know?'

'Yes.' Paul must have rung her before ringing him.

'It's going to be wonderful,' Sandra said. 'It's going to be very, very special.'

'Yes,' Andy agreed, 'it is.'

Aaron rang while he was having lunch. The connection was even worse than when Sandra called. So much so Aaron sounded like he was talking in slow motion. Andy, still surprised by the fact Priest had rung at all, could hardly believe it when he asked, 'You coming to the stadium tonight?'

'I'm in the band, remember?' Andy told him. 'Of course I'm coming to the stadium tonight.'

'We're sending a limo,' Aaron said in that deep, boomy, echoing, slow-motion voice.

'Yes, I know.'

'See you there,' promised Aaron and hung up, leaving Andy to wonder what all that was about.

His doorbell buzzed promptly on the stroke of six o'clock. Andy tweaked back the curtains and looked down. Sure enough, there was a black Merc parked in the courtyard with a uniformed chauffeur leaning on the bonnet. He was looking up towards Andy's window as if he knew exactly where to find his passenger.

As Andy reached for his coat, a memory of the last phone conversation floated through his mind. *We're sending a limo,'* Aaron Priest had said. Not Paul's sending a limo. Not *they're* sending a limo. *We're* sending a limo, as if he'd somehow got himself involved with the management of Windstorm.

Maybe he had, thought Andy sourly. Maybe that's why Priest and Campbell wore the same cinnamon aftershave.

TWENTY-NINE

To begin with, the driver might as well have been a deaf mute for all the conversation Andy got out of him. He was a big man with high cheekbones that gave an Oriental cast to his features and he looked frankly dangerous. After a few half-hearted attempts, Andy left him alone.

The limo was everything Paul Campbell promised. Andy reclined in a back seat that felt larger than a football field. While there was no Pepsi in the bar and he couldn't figure out how the television set worked, he was still impressed. A sliding panel cut him off from the driver, but an intercom allowed them to talk if he could persuade the man to say anything. Andy noticed there was a switch marked PRIVACY beside the intercom, presumably to make sure the driver didn't hear when you were talking business.

It was growing dark and the driver switched on the headlights as he pulled off the motorway. Within minutes Andy started to notice the posters. At first they just promoted the concert with a blow-up of an old photo of the *Gravediggers* in action – the same posters he'd already seen around town. Then they changed to a different poster that gave directions to the stadium.

Although he was early, there was already a serious traffic build-up.

'Don't worry, sir, we'll get you there on time,' a gruff voice said on the intercom. 'We're not going by the main route.' Andy was so surprised he jumped.

The limo pulled into a minor road and, as the chauffeur had promised, the traffic quickly thinned to nothing. Andy stared out of the window a little anxiously, hoping it wasn't going to rain. He assumed Kersten Stadium was covered, but he hadn't actually thought to ask. Surely nobody in their right mind would risk a concert in an open-air stadium at this time of year?

As it happened, the weather proved a groundless worry. There was no sign of rain by the time the limo pulled up in front of a high pair of wrought-iron gates and stopped. Andy waited as the driver got out and opened them with a key.

'Side entrance,' he explained as he climbed back in. 'Means you can avoid the fans.'

'Will they be here already?'

'Word I got from Mr Campbell is they're turning up in their thousands,' the driver volunteered. 'Afraid I mightn't be able to keep them all away from you.'

'No problem,' Andy said truthfully. Maybe when he'd been a rock superstar for thirty years he'd try to avoid his fans, but this was his first concert. He wanted to be mobbed.

As the car pulled into the tree-lined drive, Andy could see the lights of the stadium in the distance and felt a thrill of anticipation. Even at this distance he could hear rock music. He lowered the window. 'Who's the group?' he asked.

The driver actually cracked a smile. 'It's your group, Mr Clarke. The *Gravediggers*. That's the single you cut. Mr Campbell's playing it through the public sound system.'

And so it was! 'Light My Fire' as sung by Aaron Priest, lead singer of the *Gravediggers*! It was incredible, but it was happening. Andy sank back into the leather upholstery and wondered if the others felt as happy as he did.

The drive opened out into a broad, pebbled area surrounding a high semi-circular building. As the limo pulled to a halt, the driver ran round and opened Andy's door. 'Quick as you can, sir, before they spot you.'

Andy caught the sense of urgency and climbed quickly from the car. Even over the pounding music he could hear the sound of a massive crowd somewhere on the other side of the stadium.

'Andy, my man! I thought you were lost!' Paul Campbell was bearing down on him. 'Come on – the others are inside.'

From somewhere to the side a girl's voice called out, 'There's one of them!' At once a screaming crowd surged round the corner. Before he knew what was happening, Andy found himself manhandled by Campbell and the driver into the building. The driver slammed the door in the face of the screaming fans.

'Phew!' Campbell grinned. 'It looks like we're on a winner. Ever get that sort of reaction from your fans?'

'Never,' Andy told him truthfully. The appearance of the screaming crowd had unnerved him a little. For the first time he could appreciate why pop stars had bodyguards. He realised Paul Campbell was looking at him strangely. 'What? What is it?'

Campbell's eyes seemed suddenly very large and moist. 'Are you enjoying yourself, Andy?' he asked soberly. 'Can you feel the excitement?'

Andy blinked. 'Sure. Yes, wow, definitely.'

'Can you feel the energy?' Campbell asked.

Andy nodded. 'I can feel that all right.'

'Are you enjoying yourself very, very much?'

Andy felt his forehead crease into a frown. The questions seemed more than a little odd. As did Paul Campbell's expression. He looked like someone holding himself back with an enormous effort, holding himself back from an intense pleasure.

Andy said quietly, 'Yes, I'm enjoying myself.' In fact, he was beginning to feel quite uncomfortable.

Paul Campbell smiled broadly and slowly, sensuously, licked his lips. The smell of cinnamon surrounding him was almost overpowering.

THIRTY

After that another set of images flashed through Andy's mind.

Their dressing-room was the ultimate ego trip. There were life-sized blow-ups of each member of the group around the walls. There were ceiling to floor mirrors. There were miniatures of the advertising posters and a gigantic banner strung from the ceiling that said, GOOD LUCK, GRAVE-DIGGERS. There was a full-sized liquor bar with, get this, its own barman in a bow tie and a floral waistcoat.

Andy stared in astonishment, part of his mind wondering where the pictures had been taken. He didn't recognise the one of himself at all. Tim and Dave were drinking beer. They looked as stunned as Andy himself.

'Where are the others?' Andy asked.

'Sandra's got a dressing-room of her own,' Dave said.

'What about Aaron?'

Dave shrugged. 'He's around.'

Andy, in a sudden panic, remembered they hadn't checked their sound equipment. Hadn't even set up their sound equipment.

Tim smiled at him benignly. 'Chill out, cousin,' he said in a soft, phoney Kansas accent. 'It's all taken care of.' He sounded just a little drunk.

'We've got people to do that sort of thing for us now,' Dave said, smiling broadly. He sounded a little drunk as well.

'You lot decent?' Sandra's voice.

'Come in, darling,' Dave called out magnanimously.

Sandra came in, looking stunning. She was wearing the tightest of tight blue jeans with a white blouse open almost to her waist. She no longer looked tired or ill. Even her pallor seemed to be improved.

'Have you seen the size of the audience?' she asked.

Andy shook his head. 'Not yet.'

'Millions!' Sandra told them. 'Somebody told me there are more outside. Kids turned up without tickets. Paul's making arrangements to pipe the music through to them.' She giggled. 'Only way to stop a riot.'

'I'm worried about Aaron. We're on in a minute.' This from Andy.

'He's around,' Dave said. 'I saw him earlier.

Paul Campbell came into the dressing-room without knocking. He held up one hand and spread his fingers. 'Five minutes. Everybody ready?'

'Paul ...' Andy said. 'What about our guest stars?'

Campbell grinned broadly. 'They're here. We've got them hidden away in the cellar. Can't let the fans see them too soon.'

'How about letting us see them, Paul?'

'One of our guys had an idea about that,' Campbell said. 'You come out and do your first couple of opening numbers, warm the place up. Then you, Andy, or better yet Aaron, since he's up front, do a little bit of business about how the management have a couple of old friends coming on. I mean, he teases the audience a little since they all know there are going to be guest stars. Aaron builds up the mystery element, know what I mean? Tells everybody nobody knows who the guests are. Even he doesn't know who the guests are. Strings it out, gets everybody really excited. Then, when the boys *do* come on it's completely spontaneous. The crowd sees your reaction, your surprise.'

'Great idea, Paul,' said Sandra softly before Andy could answer.

'Work for you, Andy?' Campbell asked pleasantly.

Instead of answering directly, Andy asked, 'Where is Aaron anyway? I haven't seen him at all.'

Campbell shrugged. 'He's about.'

For some reason and no reason, Andy knew with absolute certainty that Aaron Priest was at that moment with the two mystery guest rock stars. He didn't know how he knew, but he knew. He felt his anger rising. How come Priest got to meet the guests when nobody else did?

But he couldn't say anything, of course. He was sure Campbell would simply deny it.

A young man stuck his head round the dressing-room door. 'You're on, boys and girl!'

'Where the hell is Aaron?' Andy asked angrily of no one in particular.

'He's waiting for you in the wings, Mr Clarke,' the young man said.

He needed a loo. He needed a loo more badly than he'd ever needed anything in his life. Campbell himself was on stage, winding up the audience as he made the introductions. From where he was standing, Andy could see only a small segment of the auditorium, but it was jammed. The hum of anticipation rose and fell like the sound of bees, sometimes growing so much it almost drowned out Campbell's words. The place felt very, very hot.

Andy looked at the others. With the exception of Priest, who seemed laid-back and cool, they were wired and intense.

'. . . latest, greatest stars of rock 'n' roll,' Paul Campbell was saying, his voice rising. 'The ones you've come to see – the *Grave. . .diggers*!'

Then they were trotting on stage to a screaming roar of appreciation and Andy suddenly found he didn't need a loo at all.

137

THIRTY-ONE

The first two numbers were instrumentals. Andy had planned it that way mainly to give everybody a chance to settle in, but the audience loved them. The buzz was incredible. Paul Campbell had taken a seat in the front row surrounded by screaming youngsters and actually looked as if he was enjoying it.

Andy looked out across the vast sea of faces and realised he'd come home. This was what he wanted to do. This was what he'd always wanted to do. People talked about the money and the fame, but this was where the real kicks were, playing your heart out while the fans screamed their appreciation.

The last chord died away, Andy counted a ten-beat silence then Aaron Priest, right on cue, bounded over to wrestle the main mike from its stand. 'Baby,' he said, holding the mike so close he might have been eating it, 'won't you light ... my fire?'

Tim hit the rhythm hard. Sandra and Andy came in pounding in perfect unison on their guitars. Then Dave picked up light and delicate on the keyboards as Priest launched the oldie that was the *Gravediggers*' first single.

The audience went wild.

In that instant, Andy knew everything was going to be all right. The group was going to be all right. The concert and the recording was going to be all right. Even his relationship with Sandra was going to be all right, although he didn't know how. The gigs he'd played before were nothing like this. The kids packing Kersten Stadium howled and stamped and waved, sending out an energy that swept Andy all the way to heaven as he played.

Paul Campbell was smiling. His teeth looked very long and sharp.

When the number finished, there was so much noise from the fans that Priest couldn't make himself heard. But after a while the audience calmed down enough for him to start his banter about the guests. Andy watched him with an odd, growing sense of unease. At first he couldn't place where it was coming from, then realised it had nothing to do with Priest at all. It was the expression on Paul Campbell's face that was making Andy uneasy.

Campbell was still smiling. It was a smile of expectation.

'You don't know who they are,' Aaron Priest was saying, referring to the mystery guests. 'The group don't know who they are. Even I don't know who they are.' He paused, grinned, then belted out, 'But now we're all going to find out! Bring on the mystery guests!' He spun round, his arm outstretched dramatically.

In that instant Andy's stomach knotted. He felt a wave of fear beyond anything he had ever experienced before. He took half a step forward, his mouth already forming the word *No!*

But then they were walking on to the stage. The stars Campbell had promised. Andy recognised the first of them at once. The long, gentle face, the granny spectacles, were unmistakable. Behind him, strutting, grinning, shirtless was the representative from *Queen*. Behind them both was someone Andy didn't recognise, a gaunt man dripping water.

'Nooooo!' wailed Andy. For some reason it did not occur to him to disbelieve what he was seeing. He would have known those first two figures anywhere: John Lennon, shot to death in 1980; Freddie Mercury who succumbed to an AIDS-related illness at the very height of his career.

And suddenly Andy knew the third figure was the member of the *Rolling Stones* that Campbell promised. Not Jagger, or course, but guitarist Brian Jones who died mysteriously in his swimming pool on 3rd July 1969.

'Noooo!' Andy wailed again, but no sound emerged. He tried to move, but could not. His eyes flickered to Sandra, Tim and Dave. They were smiling and applauding.

Then Aaron Priest came bounding back. 'I am the Lizard King,' he announced, smiling broadly. 'I can do *anything*!' As if to emphasise the boast, he reached out with his free hand and stroked Sandra's hair. She flinched, but did not move away.

'Leave her alone!' Andy screamed in sudden revulsion, but the words refused to pass his lips.

A ghastly conviction had erupted in his mind. Aaron Priest didn't just *look* like Jim Morrison. Aaron Priest really *was* Jim Morrison.

But Jim Morrison is dead, the familiar voice echoed in his head. Andy knew it was true. Jim Morrison had died in Paris on Friday 2nd July 1971 at the age of 27 years, just about the age that Aaron Priest looked right now. He died in his bath of a heart attack after a short, explosive career marked just as much by drugs and booze as rock success.

Andy knew it was true, but didn't care. It was as if something had suddenly opened up inside him to present an absolute, unquestioned certainty. The thing on stage stroking Sandra's hair was the original Lizard King himself. Like John Lennon, Freddie Mercury and Brian Jones, Jim Morrison was back from the grave.

Back from the grave and singing.

THIRTY-TWO

Andy remembered his dream. He felt the same terror, the same horror and something like the same paralysis. Was he dreaming now?

From somewhere came the memory that you couldn't feel pain in a dream – the reason why people pinched themselves to make sure they were not dreaming. Andy pinched himself now, viciously, and felt the pain. This was no dream. This was a ghastly reality.

But it was a reality in which only he appeared to notice anything amiss. Tim, Dave and Sandra were all stirring up a little background melody as Aaron Priest/Jim Morrison introduced the guests. The audience were screaming, stamping and applauding as if the names announced did not belong to dead men. What was happening here? What was going on?

Andy suddenly became aware Paul Campbell was watching him. Watching him with obvious amusement. Another segment of his dream returned to him: Campbell in black vinyl. Andy stood staring, a mixture of emptiness and panic churning his stomach. Paul Campbell knew exactly what was going on.

Morrison/Priest caressed the microphone like

a lover and announced, 'Nobody Gets Out Of Here Alive'! It was another old *Doors* number, but for Andy it was more like a prediction of the Apocalypse. He shivered. Below him in his front row seat, Paul Campbell applauded wildly. 'Featuring,' the Morrison/Priest thing went on, 'that incredible new discovery, the coming kings of rock and roll, your favourites and mine, the *Gravediggers*.' He paused for one dramatic beat, then added, with a nod and smile towards the three other animated corpses, 'And friends!'

Dave picked out a light, pleasing little refrain on his keyboards. Tim began to lay down a heavy beat on drums.

Andy let his guitar drop to the floor. His initial shocked paralysis had been replaced by gut-wrenching terror, but he still somehow managed to cross the stage and vault down into the auditorium. Fans reached out excitedly to touch him as he confronted Campbell.

'What ... have ... you ... done ... to ... them?' he asked between rasping breaths.

Campbell favoured him with a smile of almost unbelievable malice. 'What's your guess, Andy?'

Andy glanced back at the smiling faces and blank eyes of his friends. The only thing he could think of was drugs. But the entire audience was clapping and cheering the dead rock stars as if nothing was amiss. Campbell could not possibly have drugged them all.

It was as if Campbell read his thoughts. He looked at Andy and smiled. 'Nothing nearly so crude, dear boy.' The smile turned to a laugh and the sound seemed to travel through the depths of some alien dimension. 'Most of them aren't here at all.'

There was a click inside Andy's head and suddenly the stadium was deathly quiet. Andy looked slowly, fearfully around. The inside of the hall was an empty, decaying ruin, a jumble of rubble and broken seats. Peeling walls were punctuated with high smashed windows, boarded up.

There was the remains of a stage, but no sign at all of any recording equipment. Dave and Tim were frozen in curious positions. Dave was standing hands out as if about to play the keyboards, but there were no keyboards there. Tim squatted in front of a set of imaginary drums. They were both smiling vacantly. Sandra was staring out over the empty, rubble-strewn auditorium, her eyes blank.

Andy's heart began to thump wildly. This couldn't be happening. He was finding it difficult to breathe. There were no more than half a dozen lights overhead, a line of bulbs hanging from bare flexes over the stage. They were dusty and flyblown and their dim light left most of the rest of the hall in gloom.

He took a step backwards and felt glass crunch beneath his feet.

'Our kind were always masters of illusion,' Campbell said. 'One of the reasons so few people actually believe in us.'

Andy glanced behind him again. Up on the makeshift stage he could see Priest and the three guest stars for what they really were. It was a hideous sight.

144

'Won't you go up and join them?' Campbell asked. 'The *real* concert's just about to begin.'

Without thought or hesitation, Andy hurled himself towards the creature that had masqueraded as Paul Campbell. At once he found his arms gripped tightly. The sinister driver of his limo had materialised on his right. Andy glanced to his left and saw an exact twin of the same figure holding him there. He struggled furiously, but could not break free.

'This is another illusion!' he screamed at Campbell. 'They're not really here at all.'

Campbell favoured him with a mock sad smile. 'You're quite right, Andy, but isn't it interesting that it doesn't make the slightest difference? You *know* it's an illusion, but while you see it, you simply can't break free.'

Andy redoubled his efforts. He jerked and twisted, swore at Campbell, even tried to kick out.

The illusion held him in an iron grip.

THIRTY-THREE

Breathlessly, Andy stopped struggling. The grip on his arms eased at once, but he knew it would return the instant he made a move towards Paul Campbell. Andy made no move. 'Why?' he whispered. 'Why did you do this to us?'

'Do what, Andy?' Campbell asked. 'This is your big break! You'll be playing with the stars!'

'I won't be playing with anybody!' Andy snapped. 'Nor will the *Gravediggers* – we're leaving!'

'I don't think so,' Campbell said. He waved a casual hand. At once the twin drivers vanished, but Andy felt every muscle in his body grow rigid and almost deathly cold. What was happening now? He could no longer move. Even his breathing had become laboured from the sheer effort needed to raise his chest. Another illusion, but, like the drivers, one he could not break.

Campbell stood up and took his arm. 'If you won't play, perhaps you'll sit and talk with me,' he said gently.

With Campbell's hand on his arm . . .

. . . *a hand that burned and fizzled and caused darting stabs of pain* . . .

. . . Andy could move again, but only to do

146

what Campbell wanted. He sat on one of the few seats that remained intact near the front of this vast empty auditorium. As the hand was removed, he became immobile again.

From the corner of his eye, Andy could see Paul Campbell was changing. His head was elongating, his eyes transforming into featureless orbs that glittered red and feral. He looked old beyond belief, a creature from the ancient times who should have been long dead when the pyramids were built. The stench of cinnamon was almost overpowering.

'Well, isn't this jolly?' Campbell said in a voice that had become cracked and dry. He turned towards Andy. 'If you won't play, we'll have to hold the concert without you, you know.' When Andy didn't answer, he gave a mocking shrug, turned to the stage and called out, 'Let's hit it!'

'Nobody,' the Morrison thing repeated on the stage, 'Gets Out Of Here Alive!' Beside him, Sandra stood stock still as the things pretending to be Lennon, Jones and Mercury shuffled round her in an obscene dance.

Why? Andy asked himself in desperation. He was beginning to understand a great deal now. The cinnamon smell from Priest and Campbell marked them as two of a kind. So too did the native earth they kept in their refrigerators. The coffin in Priest's flat was no harmless eccentricity. Doubtless Campbell owned one too. They were creatures of the grave, creatures who had sold their souls for life eternal. They were humanity's oldest nightmare. They were vampires.

But for all he understood, Andy did not understand at all what he was doing here. He did not understand why the creatures had created this elaborate illusion. Why Priest had pretended to be a rock singer, why Campbell had become a record company executive. He did not understand why they had staged this charade. Vampires were supposed to drink human blood to sustain their undead state. But this went far beyond the ancient legends.

Once again the thing that was Paul Campbell showed its ability to read his mind. The elongated head turned towards him. 'This is my nature,' it said in a voice that reverberated from primeval depths. 'Once, long ago, I fed on blood. Now I feed on pain.' It looked away again, but continued to speak. 'An atrocity here, a war or two there – these things sustain me.' Suddenly it giggled. 'But now and then I like to snack.'

It was the most chilling thing he had ever heard. This creature, this ancient, ancient vampire, was prepared to work for weeks, to weave its illusory spells, to carry him to the heights of expectation, then dash his hopes completely . . . just to taste his pain!

Andy knew he had to move, knew he had to break away from this nightmare, knew he had – somehow – to stop the obscenity that was gathering momentum on the stage. He tried to shout, but no sound came. He tried to leap from his wooden chair, but could not. Nothing restrained him, yet he sat beside the hunched, distorted form of the old vampire like one roped and chained.

THIRTY-FOUR

On stage the three human members of the *Gravediggers* began to move as if playing their familiar instruments. Although no instruments were there, Andy heard the music, faintly at first but growing louder, the familiar, heady, pounding beat of rock and roll. He knew he was listening to the vampires' illusion, but the realisation did not change a single note.

The rotting corpse of Jim Morrison began to strut.

Andy concentrated. If he could move just one thing – an arm, a hand, even a finger – perhaps that might be enough to break the spell. His right hand was jammed into his jacket pocket and he concentrated on that. At least if he did move, Campbell might not notice.

The thing beside him did not even move its head this time. 'Go ahead, Andrew,' it said. 'Try as best you can.'

It was his mother's phrase, right down to the use of the name Andrew rather than Andy. Andy felt a welling despair. How could anyone stand against a creature that read your thoughts and knew your entire past? But he kept trying all the same.

On stage, Jim Morrison launched into the number with all the power and verve that made him famous in his lifetime. His voice was much more ragged now – perhaps the vocal cords were beginning to rot – but nobody seemed to notice. At one point he half turned as if he were singing just for Sandra.

In the pocket, Andy's fingers twitched. He savagely suppressed a surge of hope, terrified the creature beside him would feel it and once again read his mind. But Campbell, hunched and twisted, was watching the stage. Andy's fingers moved again, curling of their own accord round a coin in his jacket pocket. If he could have frowned, he would have. He never carried coins in his jacket – all his loose change went into a trouser pocket. But then, all of a sudden, the realisations hit him.

The first realisation was that his fingers had not touched a coin at all. They were curled round the medallion Snuff gave him. The second realisation was that cheap and nasty though it appeared to be, this medallion contained power beyond anything he would ever have dreamed possible. It flowed through his fingers into his arms, releasing the paralysis in his body, freeing all his locked-up muscles, sending a surge of energy that must have been a thousand times more powerful than a cocaine hit. *A Blessing For Your Goodness.*

With the energy came the third realisation, the most important one of all. Under the influence of the medallion, Campbell's illusions could not hold. What had Snuff said? – *It may help you see things the way they really are.*

One of the things he was seeing now was Campbell seated beside him, no longer the grotesque, dramatic alien fiend, but something altogether smaller and, in a curious way, more pitiable. He was like a little shrivelled-up old man. No wonder this was a creature who sometimes liked to snack. There was nothing else in his entire existence.

Andy moved.

He crashed from his chair and bounded on to the stage. The thing that had once been Jim Morrison was reaching out again to stroke Sandra's hair. Andy grabbed the arm and gagged as it ripped off with a dry, crackling sound like paper tearing. He stared for a moment, then threw it to one side and smashed bodily into the Morrison thing, sending it flying.

He grabbed Sandra's hand. 'Come on, Sandra! Come on, Dave! Come on, Tim!' he screamed. 'We have to get out of here!'

Dave turned dreamily towards him. 'Oh, hey, Andy, you've arrived. I was worried, man.'

'Come *on*!'

Something of the urgency in his voice seemed to reach them, for they turned to follow as he dragged Sandra towards the edge of the stage. They moved slowly, but at least they moved. Andy found himself facing the ancient vampire again, now no longer the shrunken, pathetic, childlike creature he had seen under the first surge of power from the medallion, but a thing once again disguised as Paul Campbell at his most smooth, most fashionable, most trendy.

'You're not going anywhere,' Campbell said.

Andy hit him, catching Campbell squarely on the jaw. The man was lighter than he looked, so light that the blow actually lifted him off his feet which caused him to fall backwards off the stage.

The scene changed to slow motion. Andy watched in surging horror as Campbell described a graceful arc through the air, then crashed into one of the wooden chairs on which he and Andy had been sitting. The chair smashed on impact and the wood splintered. Andy watched wide-eyed as an enormous shard emerged from Campbell's chest like a stake. Campbell convulsed violently, heels drumming as he struggled to get free. Then blood gushed suddenly from his mouth, he twitched once and was still. Whatever power had inhabited him was gone.

'What's happening? Where are we?' Tim asked. Both he and Dave were looking around them like awakened sleepwalkers.

'Get out of here!' Andy screamed urgently. They were still far from safe despite Campbell's death. The undead creatures on the stage were shuffling towards them in a rotting, putrid mass. The whole hall was filled with the stench of cinnamon; the stench of corruption.

Dave glanced over his shoulder then took off like a scalded rabbit. Tim took one look, screamed and followed him. They negotiated the rubble like cross-country runners and disappeared from the hall. Andy wanted nothing more than to follow them, but he still had Sandra to think of. She seemed dazed and listless.

'Come on!' Andy shouted in her ear. He

grabbed her hand and half dragged her from the stage. Together they stumbled towards the exit.

Andy glanced behind him only once. The group of dead rockers was still following them, but fortunately moving slowly. With a feeling of revulsion Andy noticed Lennon's foot had fallen off and he was moving in erratic circles on the stump.

Andy half pushed Sandra through the door and slammed it behind them. There was no lock or bolt on the outside but he shifted a packing-case half full of metal junk across the entrance. It would not hold the undead long, but it might hold them long enough.

He looked around. For some reason the outside appearance of the stadium was even more shocking than the mess inside. The pebbledash was chipped and cracked and flaked, a drainpipe hung out drunkenly and there was lichen on the walls. Old fuel drums were rusting over by one wall. Somebody long ago had carved the words JEANNIE PRESTON DOES IT at shoulder height on the door.

Andy groaned and began, inwardly, to pray. Then he ran towards the fuel drums.

At his side, Sandra gasped, 'What are you going to do?' It was the first time she'd spoken since he'd dragged her from this cursed hall and he felt a surge of relief. He'd started to wonder if the shock of her experience might have affected her mind.

Andy stopped and gripped her by the shoulders. 'I'm going to set fire to the building,' he told her firmly. 'You can help. We've got to destroy those things in there!'

Sandra drew back in horror. 'No,' she whispered. 'You can't!'

'They're not alive!' Andy hissed. 'They're not even *real*. That's not John and Brian and Freddie in there. Those are just bodies, just animated, rotting bodies cloaked in an illusion. We must destroy them!'

'No,' Sandra whispered again. Behind her he saw the packing-case shift slightly as the pressure on the door began to build.

'All right,' Andy said. 'It doesn't matter. I'll do it myself.' Before she could stop him, he turned and raced the last few steps to the fuel drums, praying they still contained something flammable.

He hit the first one running but it skittered away from him, empty. Without even stopping to think, he grabbed the second. It was heavy, obviously full, and he switched his prayer to a plea that it should not be full of water. But as he pushed it over, his nose told him at once his prayers were answered. The drum spilled a pool of black oil that flowed towards the building.

Matches! He'd carried matches since that awful day in Aaron Priest's flat, but he wasn't sure he'd switched them over when he changed his jacket. He scrabbled in the pocket. No matches! The undead were pounding on the door now. He could see the packing-case move again, inch by inch.

He found the matches in a trouser pocket. The first one flared, then died. He struck another and another, flinging them towards the river of oil. Two hit the liquid and, astonishingly, went out. The third flared.

Andy grabbed Sandra's hand and raced, half dragging her, away from the building. She seemed stunned, wide-eyed, still muttering 'No, no, no!' He had to get her clear. He knew exactly what would happen if the other drums contained the same fuel as the first. As he ran he prayed Dave and Tim would be far enough away.

He leaped a low wall, flung himself flat and pulled Sandra down with him. In his mind's eye he could see the river of burning oil race towards the building. The old structure caught at once and began to burn fiercely. Then the flames reached the remaining fuel drums...

There was a dull *clump*, not at all like the special effects explosions produced for the thriller movies. But the flames flared so high he could see them reflected redly on the clouds above. Andy sat up. It was even better than he'd hoped. The whole of Kersten Stadium was on fire. Thick black smoke rolled skywards. He could see, silhouetted in the flames, figures thrashing around as they fought to escape.

None did. In minutes it was over, although the building continued to burn fiercely. Andy felt relief roll across him like a tidal wave. Paul Campbell was no more. The animated corpses were reduced to ashes. And if the immediate hopes of the *Gravediggers* were in ashes too, that was preferable to the horror that had gone before.

'It's over,' he said quietly, turning towards Sandra.

But the thing beside him was no longer Sandra. It was a creature of leather skin and rotting limbs. Its hand gripped his with hellish intensity. Its mouth was pulled back in a grotesque rictus as it murmured, 'Andy, darling, you shouldn't have burned our friends.'

Andy tried to back away then, tried to jerk away in panic, but the thing would not release his hand. One of its eyes popped suddenly as a blind white worm crawled out. As he stared at the worm, he found himself remembering the night they had kissed and the cloaked figure in the alleyway across her road. It had been Priest, of course, coming for his nightly feed.

It all made sense now. Her look of illness, her pallor, the intermittent scent of cinnamon. Priest had fed from her, infected her. Gradually, Sandra had become a vampire too. Now, like Morrison, she was trying to cover her identity in the cloak of an illusion.

Andy's breath was coming in short, spasmodic gasps. 'Who are you?'

'Janis,' said the thing a little crossly, as if he should have known. 'I'm Janis Joplin.'

Janis Joplin was the queen of rock and roll. She took an overdose of drugs and died on 4th October 1970.

Andy Clarke tried vainly to remove his hand from hers and felt his universe begin to dim.